I0838199

SHOES

STEVEN PAUL LANSKY

DOS MADRES

2025

DOS MADRES PRESS INC.

P.O. Box 294, Loveland, Ohio 45140

www.dosmadres.com   editor@dosmadres.com

Dos Madres is dedicated to the belief that the small press is essential to the vitality of contemporary literature as a carrier of the new voice, as well as the older, sometimes forgotten voices of the past. And in an ever more virtual world, to the creation of fine books pleasing to the eye and hand.

Dos Madres is named in honor of Vera Murphy and Libbie Hughes, the "Dos Madres" whose contributions have made this press possible.

Dos Madres Press, Inc. is an Ohio Not For Profit Corporation and a 501 (c) (3) qualified public charity. Contributions are tax deductible.

Executive Editor: Robert J. Murphy

Illustration & Book Design: Elizabeth H. Murphy
www.illusionstudios.net

Drawings, paintings & photos by Steven Paul Lansky

Typeset in Adobe Garamond Pro Warnock Pro
ISBN 978-1-962847-26-1
Library of Congress Control Number: 2025937042

About the Cover Image:
SIX WAITING FOR A SEVENTH–YOU, THE VIEWER
Homemade gouache, ink, oil, pencil, and marker on paper,
16.5 x 30", Generated circa 1982
From the Private Collection of the artist Steven Paul Lansky

Each of the figures appears in individual portraits by the artist. In this case they are gathered bringing gifts. From right to left: Dianne is bringing music, Michael brings tobacco leaves, Jane has a handmade oak rocker, Dan's hands are full of jewels and beads, Rachel carries fabric, and Hendrik offers weapons. Each of these figures was a part of the artist's life, and each brought him something intangible. The painting was a way of acknowledging the gifts by having them represent basic commodities. Under a gas lamp, the six, gather to see what you, the viewer brings to them. The painting is on two pieces of paper connected with paper clips out of view because of the frame.

for Uncle

FOREWORD

Lansky's singular, marvelously absurd, graphic, hybrid novella, *Shoes* has cutting-edge detailed, prose modeled on recanted reality. It moves like the doorway god Janus, who, upon the threshold, looks both outwards, and to the interior. Two faces, toggle facets of moments, the third eye drawn from both, or either, and between the front and back, the edge. Imaginary and real, fantastic and mundane, possibilities sublimely rendered in comedic instants tucked into the mind as wayposts.

The novella shifts between places, a possible diagnosis, a change of heart, and/or venue, that keeps the reader in a rather delightful attempt to keep up with or abandon meaning in a literal sense. Take the rich detail and let the author's sure hand move the narrative smartly back and forth through the doorway. Understand that the instrument of illustration is unnecessary for genuine pleasure in getting a little lost in the story and getting a little lost in the author, but the graphic element helps. There is a personal metaphor in all the mileage piled up, in the distance, from place to place recounted, time travel, from footnote to footnote.

Steve Lansky has a unique perspective, from the doorward gaze, drawn either way, of the neurotypical, or the neurospectacular. Somewhere in between ambition, and accomplishment (something of a bipolarity itself, eh?). He starts a conversation with a version of himself, and flexes outward, as the reader becomes the most colorful of chameleons. Sure, there's some shapeshifting here, and a relaxation of the serotonin guardrails, that order memory, and experience, to behave in a linear way, but it's supposed to be fickle.

I found the chapter titled, *Halfway House*, to be a wonderful rendition of the overall theme music. The harmonica is rendered as its most laconic atmosphere. It has a memory that tastes like the box the years came in. (see Moby Grape- *Listen, my friends, I'm yours forever, listen, my friends, I won't leave you ever*)

The footnotes on the negotiations of the *battle of the tables* were such a perfect insert, to illustrate the march of hallucination, that becomes the history of an event, after everyone, with a memory of it gone. The proposed setting is the nature of perception. Even-handedness is at its best incarnation, where the exchange of the sane, and the imaginary across the same space, glare incredulously at each other.

This is a book you will find easy to read. On one hand, it is a travel narrative that moves through layers of history and space. Here are familial gangster-kindled koans, old beach vistas, strange relatives, and people with wonderful names. Bicycles, cars, airplanes, Greyhounds, and thumbs crisscross the neural maps—places you can only find through the author's plan of the oft-unplanned. A recount demanded!

Peace, on the other hand, in the narrator's mind, is a sticky, messy affair that we code with the restless truth of self-doubt, the enigma of memory, the placation of grift, guilt, and potential harm to oneself and others—a comedy in the error of some odd gene editing by the great bean counter.

—KEN KAWAJI
poet emeritus, Kaldi's Coffeehouse Bookstore

SHOES

I RUSHED THROUGH THE HOUSE, my face twisted, pulling long fingers through shaggy, shoulder-length, brown hair.

"Fuck this! I need shoes! Shoes!"

I took off my worn, desert boots on the porch and threw them at the woodpile, pulled off blue, cotton socks, snagging them on long, well-manicured fingernails. I had worked on my nails all morning before walking to the wedding. I drank bourbon neat, sampled champagne, listened to a string quartet and ate my fill, then walked three miles home. My father shut the screen door, its loose, aluminum frame rattling as it closed. He stood tall, white-bearded, a strap held his glasses snug to his head; my mother stood behind him.

"You can't come in," he said.

"Will you go to the Emergency Room?" she asked, her brown eyes flickering with resolve, salt and pepper hair in disarray.

I picked a four-foot-long stick off the woodpile, test swung it, then shouted, "What the fuck for? I need shoes." My jeans were torn at the knees, white threads hanging.

Need new shoes—can't come in house—don't remember— kissed the bride's mother at the reception—will you go to hospital— OK OK OK signed myself in for a couple of days—dosed with perphenazine[1]—took Minnesota Multiphasic Personality Inventory; shrink says I'm schizo—made belt in occupational therapy, then left—back home for a day—smoked joint at bike shop— extinguished it in wet paint— puffed more—walked down Clifton Ave. watching sycamores, oaks, and maples swaying in breeze and the wind, sky as if they were particles, grainy like a photograph enlarged too much—pushed beyond the mind. Struggling to walk against the wind—leaves swaying like fragments of oversized chunks of chloroform and oxygen.

---

1   Trilafon—a typical antipsychotic drug used to treat psychotic disorders such as schizophrenia

Greater Cincinnati Airport—Spring 1977

My father handed me a Rolls-Royce T-shirt, light blue with darker emblem, two capital R's intertwined, at Delta gate 6B. He had stolen it. My mother propelled me forward, gripping her ticket with white knuckles, a veiny, bulging fist. My father couldn't hug me good-bye and winced through brown, plastic-framed glasses, his eyes misting, graying from the brown.

I saw the wince and said, "When do I get the car?" low under my breath, a mutter—then louder, "a start—but I want the car."

My father rubbed his sweaty, big hands on his jeans.

I walked on the plane before Mom, pausing down the aisle, whistling *From the Halls of Montezuma*. She sat by me. I looked out the window at the heat rising off the tarmac, a lipstick oval smear on the Plexiglas, and an Alexander Calder[1] psychedelic, blue, red, yellow, and white jet that taxied in bright sunlight. The plane door closed. My ears tightened as the cabin huffed. The stewardess swung past in a tight, navy mini-skirt, natural hose and thick mauve make-up. She walked a gentle bump and grind, her hard nipples revealed through a thin, white, cotton blouse. Her brown eyes swam with sex. In my mind her black pupils stopped on my face, working their way down my body to my crotch, back up, slowed at my chin, lips, the trace of mustache. I prayed, *Lord, Lord, don't card me*, then mentally lowered her mini, revealing a dark tousle of kinky fur between her bare thighs above dimpled knees—I caught her eyes again, grinned, and licked my lips.

---

1   In 1973 Braniff International Airways commissioned American, innovative sculptor Alexander Calder to paint a DC 8 jet that was scheduled to fly between North and South America.

"Dolly Parton is on the plane and she's graciously offered a glass of wine for everyone in coach this morning," she said.

Mom looked at me, and said, "No, thank you," her olive tone returning to her hands—the pale ticket dispatched a moment back.

I said, "Red, please," and the stewardess noted on her pad.

I turned to my page again and scribbled: *Dolly Parton—free wine—I'm having red. Who is Dolly Parton? The name's familiar. We're at 30,000 feet, Mom's reading Skybeat. Going to see Aunti Zen in San Francisco, Tom in the Inner Sunset—but what really peeves me. . . .*

"Your wine, sir."

I paused, accepted the clear plexi cup and sipped generously. Mom had nothing to say nor did she look up. I was nineteen years old. I lived the adventure of my years—I wondered aloud, "Does Dolly fly Delta to San Francisco a lot?"

Mother looked up. "How would I know, Jack?" she asked.

"Where are you going to stay," I asked, "with Tom or your sister?" She didn't answer. I looked again at the pale blue T-shirt and fingered the Rolls-Royce patch in my shirt pocket.

San Francisco — May 1977

We landed in San Francisco sleepy and tipsy, now Mom propelled me to the gate where Aunti Zen appeared in loose fitting clothes—thank God she wasn't in robes—gray hair cropped close, garlic on her breath and a canvas bag over one arm.

"Good to see you, Jack," she said while managing to hold me at arm's length, look concerned and turn to her sister to see the hurt and disappointment in Mom's eyes. Her fist clenched the carry-on handle as we walked to the car. Aunti drove badly, as if she hadn't had much practice on the six- and eight-lane freeway. We snaked to Tom's place in the Inner Sunset without getting lost. There were familiar landmarks: The Pan Handle, Golden Gate Park, the N Judah streetcar, The Owl and Monkey Café. Tom, a husky, young man with thick, blond hair, welcomed me with a hug. His usual quirky grin absent, I noticed concern. Thought to milk it.

There was a flat of overripe avocados. Tom worked at Veritable Vegetables, a collective, produce warehouse in the Mission.

"Let's make guacamole, Tom," I said.

"Later, Jack," Tom said.

I sat at the green kitchen table in shadow looking through to the sun porch where a hanging marijuana plant flowered in tiers of bud. I got up, walked over, picked up a plastic spray bottle and misted the pot plant. On the vinyl table-top lay a poster promoting a Marijuana Smoke-in on the Civic Center Lawn that afternoon featuring Paul Krassner[1],

---

1   Paul Krassner was an American author, journalist, comedian, and the founder, editor and a frequent contributor to the freethought magazine *The Realist*, first published in 1958. Krassner became a key figure in the counterculture of the 1960s as a member

editor of *Hustler* magazine, Commissioner Harvey Milk[2], Congressman Willie Brown[3], the band Moby Grape[4] among others. I had written four erotic short stories and had sent them all to *Hustler* several weeks before. I had met Paul twice.

The first time had been with Ken Kesey[5] at Wilma's place in Palo Alto when Ken was passing through promoting

---

of [Ken Kesey](#)'s [Merry Pranksters](#) and a founding member of the [Yippies](#), and is even credited with coining the term as well. During Larry Flynt's born again period Krassner became editor of *Hustler*.

2	Harvey Bernard Milk was an American politician and the first openly gay elected official in the history of California, where he was elected to the San Francisco Board of Supervisors. Although he was the most pro-LGBT politician in the United States at the time, politics and activism were not his early interests; he was neither open about his sexuality nor civically active until he was 40, after his experiences in the counterculture movement of the 1960s.

3	Willie Lewis Brown Jr. is an American politician of the Democratic Party. Brown served over 30 years in the California State Assembly, spending 15 years as its speaker. He later became mayor of San Francisco, the first African American to hold that office.

4	Moby Grape is an American rock group founded in 1966, known for having all five members contribute to singing and song-writing, which collectively merged elements of folk music, blues, country, and jazz with rock and psychedelic music. They were one of the few groups of which all members were lead vocalists. The group's first incarnation ended in 1969, but they have reformed many times afterwards and continue to perform occasionally. Their name is funny.

5	Kenneth Elton Kesey was an American novelist, essayist, and countercultural figure. He considered himself a link between the Beat Generation of the 1950s and the hippies of the 1960s. Known for Acid Tests, Magic Bus Trips, and the novel: *One Flew Over the Cuckoo's Nest,* he attracted curious followers.

the Second Perennial Poetical HOOHAW![6] (I was living in Wilma's communal house. She was in her forties, had two kids that were living in the commune with different fathers, who were both absent, that had other families. She was nearly six feet tall, a striking brunette with whom I learned about alcohol, drugs and sex, more to my detriment than her credit. It was in that milieu that I began to write on my own and to meet writers who became my peers.) Krassner then grabbed a yellow, funnel-shaped child's toy, held it to his crotch pointing with his purpose, pantomimed pissing, saying, "They just invented the penis for women. You simply hold it in place, and **she** can pee wherever **he** can, making the world a more equal place." Everyone but Wilma had laughed while Krassner mock peed on the living room and finally tossed the toy across the floor, following Ken into the kitchen with total devotion.

The second time we met had been a rather anticlimactic triumph; at the HOOHAW! I gave Krassner my best hitchhiking sign. Crafted from articles collected over time, the sign was lettered with dayglo-green paint outlined in black marker, and it folded in the center with carefully cut strips of rubber tire screwed into the plywood to form hinges. *Cosmic Hitchhiking Law #1 states that the amount of time spent making a sign is inversely proportional to the amount of time it takes to get a ride.* The HOOHAW! sign had delivered me from Palo Alto, California, to Eugene, Oregon, in one ride, a distance of over seven hundred miles, without being shown. Krassner had accepted it without emotion, just shook his head of brown curls and hid his eyes behind dark lenses.

The manuscripts were not returned.

---

6   HOOHAW!—a 24 hour poetical gathering in Eugene, Oregon in May 1977, hosted by Ken Kesey and including Allen Ginsberg, Jack Micheline, Rashaan Roland Kirk, The Flying Karamazov Brothers, et al.

I washed my hands in the kitchen sink, dried them on a towel that hung on the fridge handle, pointed to the poster, raised my eyebrows.

"Veritable Vegetables is trucking in the stage," Tom said to me out of Mom's range. "Not a word." I nodded. The deception bothered me.

The Halfway House

I walked into the milieu, my typed manuscript under one arm, and a stack of hardbound sketchbooks under the other. I believed the rapidograph in my shirt pocket identified me as a serious architect of novels, novellas, drama, and poetics. Now, that's a little deluded to think a casual observer could interpret that much about me from a pen in a pocket. I sat at the oval, brown dining room table[1] looking

---

1   The mention of the oval table is an oblique reference to a sense that communication between the older generation (in this case the narrator's parents) and the younger generation had broken down. This is a bit of history about the Vietnam War negotiations: These discussions, which began in November 1968, were centered on questions about the shape of the conference table, how many tables there should be, and how they would be placed. These discussions became known as the 'battle of the tables' and would last ten weeks until mid-January 1969 as fighting continued to rage and Richard Nixon won the presidential election. From the start, it was recognized that a triangular table (with the North Vietnamese/NLF combined but the US and South Vietnamese separate) would be a non-starter as it would imply that the Communist side was outnumbered two-to-one. North Vietnam wanted a square table in order to provide further legitimacy to the NLF, and also suggested four tables arranged in either a circular or a diamond pattern. The American preference was for a two-sided table or two rectangular tables. The North Vietnamese countered by suggesting a round table. Whereas the Americans supported the idea of a round table on the basis that people sitting at the table wouldn't have any position, Saigon then protested that a round table meant that everyone was equal which would imply that the NLF delegation were equal to the South Vietnamese government. As a result, the US suggested six variants of a round table, including a round table bisected with a strip of baize to provide a symbolic dividing line. Later the benefits and drawbacks of an oval table were debated but the idea eventually was rejected, as were two semi-circular tables, one round table cut in half, a 'flattened ellipse', a 'broken diamond' and a parallelogram. The Danish mathematician and designer Piet Hein proposed a super-elliptical table with golden section proportions – neither square nor

out the windows at the building right next door. I listened to a tall, thin-lipped, blonde fellow with a German accent and receding hairline who talked often, and nearly continuously, about Kafka, Jung, and Heisenberg. He did his dissertation on Kafka at Yale and marveled that I had been at Harvard. At the table sat a brunette who looked down through thick glasses. She was thin, anorexic, had badly applied, nude nail polish, and yammered about the CIA and Nixon. Later I wondered if she knew Nixon—believed she was part of his family—or more likely she had thought as much and persuaded me that it was possible with her nagging depression, interest in booze and elemental darkness. She cursed in a low voice about how they were going to get to her, take her from here, and that she didn't care as long as she didn't have to be a prisoner for long. She heaved a suicidal sigh and talked about pills, razors, death and taxes—all Nixon family concerns. I met a younger woman whose long, red hair tangled over her face hiding pimples. Her hands moved in parallel constructions as if joined by hidden strings like a marionette. When she raised the right hand to violently gesture around her head, the left hand waved along. Even in the group she whined in staccato bursts complaining she hadn't sexed enough.

After seated introductions, a woman walked into the room, blue eyes flashed like neon darts, straight, dark-brown hair past the shoulder; she was slight, sexy, and puzzling. I caught her eyes, followed them right to me; she swung around the table moving like a panther, then slowed, gently reached

---

round but midway between the two that 'would allot the two major parties 100 inches to every 6.18 for the two minor parties all the while suggesting sovereignty with alliance' (technically speaking this table would have a perimeter that satisfied the formula: $x^{2.5}+[y/a]^{2.5}=1$ where $a=[.5][\sqrt{5}-1]$).

out to me, her hand touched mine, middle finger to middle finger. Under her breath she murmured in a throaty way, "I want to fuck you." Then whirling away, hair gleaming, eyes splashing wider than I had ever seen, she was gone. Stunned, I hadn't even got her name. I stared away. "Cinder!" someone shouted after her. "I'm going to the shower," she shouted back.

The thin-lipped German had a few years on me and insisted he was better suited for Cinder. "We'll divide up the staff, you take Corrina," he said. I hadn't yet met Corrina.

Mom left without saying good-bye and Aunti Zen had said, "Call me." Nothing more. My new home had only a pay phone in the hall. Four floors—third and fourth "off limits." My room in the back smelled of sweat socks and smegma, looked dark and dusty. Two beds, no roommate. The electric typewriter on the third "off limits." "How am I supposed to write?" I asked no one in particular. The first floor had a rubber room; wrestling mats tied to the walls, a mat on the floor, hanging mats around a bare bulb with a cage around it. During the tour I spotted a fellow reading in there. *Oral Traditions in Buddhism* was the title.

Before lunchtime we had a bit of a happening. A pinch-faced woman visitor, a former resident, with a pink, knit purse that overflowed with curled paper came and read poetry. The thin German gave a brief discourse on German mysticism. The pimpled girl wore a white shirt that showed off her midriff, listened for a while then left the room. It seemed everything annoyed her. She barked and rustled her big skirt as she slipped out of the circle. The Nixon girl, dressed in a black unitard, sat rocking in a blue chair in the curved nook by the window, knees at her tiny chest, making cooing noises under her breath. I sat on the floor on some throw pillows, read from a yellow legal pad some mutterings from the flight out from Cincinnati.

A book on oral traditions—I don't like this place—I'll never finish the novel here. They could pay a lot less than three grand a month to put me up in an apartment with a typewriter. They say they won't medicate me. I think this place won't work. There's studio space though, art supplies; no sexual relations with anyone. The way they phrased it. Rules. Neither staff, nor residents. A book on oral traditions?

I found some peanut butter, a banana, and a loaf of wheat bread in the kitchen, made a sandwich, ate it, while drinking tap water with the others milling around, eating.

It wasn't much of a lunch. I put my things in my room.

"I'm going out," I announced to no one in particular. I came out the entry door after racing downstairs, checked my key to be sure it worked. The Nob Hill corner grocery advertised all night wine and beer. LATER. CIVIC CENTER LAWN IS CLOSE ENOUGH TO WALK TO TODAY. I traced my way there on this marvelous San Francisco day. A few folks were gathering on the lawn. The salute to grass came slowly, uncurling haltingly like a fettered snake, rippling altered consciousness through the growing crowd. The stage was set, and I found an older man with a beard, sunglasses and a strange T-shirt with a pink and blue, double helix down the back.

"My own design," the man said, opening a small pill bottle and sliding out a toothpick-sized cigarette. "I call it the DNA Tee." He shared smoke with me; my insides unfurled and went sailing around the lawn. When the speeches began, they all sounded like clouds of color swept across an amber sky. I heard all the headliners. The musical miasma came next, pulsing and rolling; I felt in awe of all the vibes. A naked man walked by. The crowd never noticed. I wished the man had been a woman, momentarily, then simply accepted life. After the music settled, the crowd dispersed, many drinking bottled beer, and chatting. I walked back up to Nob Hill.

Curiously enough, the next day brought many new workers, and the next, more. Inside a week I had counted twenty-two staff and students. Corrina was blond, overweight, cute and sassy, filling tight blue jeans. "Hey, Jack," she said, "I hear you play harmonica." Corrina followed me around, touched me on the arm. On the back porch we sat together. I wailed on my reeds. Corrina draped an arm over my shoulder.

A little presumptuous—the rules—then this—Corrina let me buy the joint on the way back from the store with wine. Are the rules to be bent, broken and mutilated? What about the alumnus who brought brandy—I had a snort. And Rod, the guy who brought in a foil-wrapped bit of coke that everyone tasted, Rod was staff. I like painting—the nudes—I chanted one night and painted nudes with black watercolor, the brush as dry as I could conjure. Corrina tried to kiss me last night.

Δ Δ Δ   Δ Δ Δ

Cinder proved the great mystery of the house. She was my governor of Ecotopia[1]. Smile, eyes, straight teeth, looks, all looks. "So, you're Greek?" she asked. "That's why you write books." They tried to get the residents to work communally. We resisted.

One night I told Fred, another staff, to watch my beads. I had bought them after a Greenpeace reading, where Gary Snyder[2] wowed a crowd at San Francisco Hall. A black man at a transit stop had offered pea sized gemstones, instead I purchased the beads. From the window of the N Judah streetcar, I had seen him arrested. My beads had a heavy silver ring and coke spoon. "Fred, I'm going out." Fred kind of ignored me, but I made the point real clear. "I'm going to trust you to watch my beads." I put them on the table and went out to the corner store for a can of beer. When I came in, I started on the first floor watching the pimple faced girl sit on her bed and whine. I sipped and listened.

"Nobody likes me," she whined.

"You're OK," I said.

"You just say that. **You** wouldn't kiss me. No one even wants me."

I sipped and listened.

"Nobody would even rape me," she said.

"If you want, I'd rape you," I said.

---

1   *Ecotopia*—a speculative novel by Ernest Callenbach self-published in 1975.

2   Gary Snyder is an American man of letters. Perhaps best known as a poet, he is also an essayist, lecturer, and environmental activist with anarchoprimitivist leanings. He has been described as the "poet laureate of Deep Ecology". Snyder is a winner of a Pulitzer Prize for Poetry and the American Book Award. His work, in his various roles, reflects an immersion in both Buddhist spirituality and nature. Known also as the longest surviving Beat Generation Poet, he performs his work to this day. *Turtle Island* is a favorite.

She screamed, "GET OUT! GET OUT! ANIMAL!"

I climbed upstairs, still holding the beer.

Fred had gone up to the third floor. He heard the girl yelling and went down to her room. I found the beads on the table. First off, I knew I was in trouble and Fred would believe her side. Also, I felt Fred had violated our agreement about the beads, abandoning them on the dining room table. I went to the pay phone and called the police.

Fred was downstairs talking to the girl when the police knocked on the door. He let them in as I watched from the stairwell. They looked like they were a bit tipsy, eyes rolling, hands on their clubs. "We got a call there's a domestic dispute?" the short, blond one said.

"I called, sir," I said.

"You Jack Acid?" the other one asked. He was big and fat; both had Irish accents. I thought to myself that I was lucky to have called and been delivered with drunken, Irish cops.

"Yeah," I said. "Fred promised to watch my jewelry and it almost got stolen."

"Who's Fred?" the short one asked.

Fred looked around, smiled at the cops, glared at me. "Jack is one of the residents."

"You live here, Fred?" the short one asked.

The girl could be heard crying through the bedroom door.

"No sir. I work here. This is a group home," Fred said.

"So." The short cop cocked his head at me. The other cop had a pocket notebook. "What can we do to help?"

"Tell him not to lie to me," I said, pointing at Fred.

"You lie to him?" The older cop looked at Fred.

Fred looked tired. He folded his arms across his chest, said, "Jack has been drinking."

"You been drinking, Jack?" the short cop asked.

"I had a beer," I said. "He still lied to me."

The two cops looked at one another and nodded. "We don't need assistance," one said on his radio. There was a bit of static, then a word of assurance.

The older cop had the last word. "Jack, you work this out with Fred here and try not to call us again tonight."

They left, swaggeringly.

Fred told me to leave for a while. I went out and bought a half-pint of bourbon. I shared the hooch with the anorexic brunette, sipping it neat. The director was out of town, but Fred called in a Jewish doctor, who was pissed to be paged from his son's wedding. The doctor listened to the laundry list of my broken rules. The doctor said, "We can take you to the hospital."

I finally agreed to go. Aunti Zen met me and the staff there. At San Francisco General, the doctor prescribed haloperidol[3]. I refused to take the medicine and was never admitted. I wandered around all night, slept for a while in an auditorium on the San Francisco State Medical school campus listening to a guy play piano; a policeman woke me and asked me to leave. In the morning I picked up my belongings at Nob Hill and took a cab to Zen Center[4].

---

3   **Haloperidol**, sold under the brand name **Haldol** among others, is a typical antipsychotic medication.[4] Haloperidol is used in the treatment of schizophrenia, tics in Tourette syndrome, mania in bipolar disorder, delirium, agitation, acute psychosis, and hallucinations in alcohol withdrawal.

4   San Francisco Zen Center— is a network of affiliated Sōtō Zen practice and retreat centers in the San Francisco Bay area, comprising City Center or Beginner's Mind Temple, Tassajara Zen Mountain Center, and Green Gulch Farm Zen Center. The sangha was incorporated by Shunryu Suzuki Roshi and a group of his American students in 1962. Today SFZC is the largest Sōtō organization in the West.

There's No Center to Zen Center

While at Zen Center, I decided to hitch down to Wilma's place in Palo Alto to sell my books. On the way down, a cold blustery day, I stopped on El Camino Real at a Rolls-Royce dealership.I walked in boldly, said, "I'd like a car."
The suited salesman ran a finger down his tie, checked me out. His cologne nearly blinded me.

"How about the green Corniche in the drive?" I asked. I had on my blue-on-blue RR T-shirt. I felt magnificent.

I had stolen my pick-up truck from Wilma after selling it to her. Somehow, looking at the Rolls, in my state of mind, I sensed no boundary between appropriate and wrong behavior. I can't exactly say I knew the Rolls was not mine, but I guess something stretched my thoughts. Wilma had told me about the Tibetan guru, who went to Harvard, with the "crazy school of wisdom," who had had some sort of Rolls-Royce incident in his youth. Why not me? I had driven the Chevy pick-up to Santa Fe, with Macho, the dog, then returned it by letting some total strangers drive it back to Wilma's. I hadn't seen Wilma, or Macho, in months.

"That's the owner's car," said the salesman.
"That's the one I want," I said.
"He'll be back in an hour." The salesman's air increased.
"I just finished my novel," I said.
"Just call your bank and I'm sure we can make a deal." The salesman grinned.

I went to the phone, took out my wallet, pretended to look for the phone number, fumbled a bit, then walked out. As I walked around the green Corniche, I saw a silver dollar on the center console. I tried the driver's door. Locked. I kept walking.

At Wilma's place, Wilma, thankfully, wasn't home. Macho growled and barked, as though I were a total stranger, or at least an enemy. A fellow who lived in the second house keyed the barn's padlock where I found my books all boxed up. I took Hesse, Kafka, Dostoyevsky, Nin, Olson, Kerouac, Snyder, Kesey, *The Sutra of Hui Neng, The Lotus Sutra,* two books on the Tao, *The Urantia Book,* and others. I kept eleven Paul Goodman books. The fellow gave me a ride into town. At the Chimera bookstore, an old Victorian house in downtown Palo Alto, I sold everything the man would buy for twenty-five dollars. I was left with *The Urantia Book, Calculus for the College Student, Random House Dictionary, Roget's Thesaurus* and a few other huge, heavy hardbacks. I managed to haul two boxes over to the Greyhound Bus Terminal before it started raining. I addressed my books: The White House, 1600 Pennsylvania Avenue, Washington, DC and left them there, heading out on thumb power in the rain.

I figured to one day get to the White House and find my books in safe keeping. I told myself I was thinking ahead. My life sank but my dreams were buoyant. These were the big books that only the truly erudite would value. Someone up there would know I was coming for them.

I thumbed to Carmel Valley by the coastal highway at first, my angular hand propped against hip, feet protesting loudly when I had to walk. In the valley the golden rolling hills sounded in my head, a song lyric. Somehow, I managed to get near Tassajara Hot Springs by late day, sun raising steam off the narrow road, the final ride on the back of a hay cutting rig to Jamesburg as far as the mail was delivered. I approached the whitepaneled house and knocked. A young fellow in loose fitting clothes appeared, mug in hand, head shaved to a fleshy shine. I introduced myself, stated I came to see Aunti Zen. The man looked surprised, asked if she expected me. I rubbed my hands together, then on my jeans, smiled, showing the gold front tooth and mumbled an answer. The man did not ask again.

"She's at Tassajara, headed out tomorrow. Want to stay and wait?"

"I'd like to go in," I said.

"No vehicles passing in tonight. You might walk in come morning— like as not they'll be on their way out before you get in." With that, he swung the door wide, invited me in for tea, fruit, to roll a cigarette. I peeled a navel orange with big hands, rolled an adequate stick, puffed and sipped green tea with milk and honey. I slept in a small bunk house.

Poppies, dirt road, stones half the size of my shoe . . . I walked toward Tassajara. Aunti Zen came out in a coupe behind Zen Master in his BMW touring car, with driver and other monks. They stopped, exchanged words, no questions . . . I got in. She was not pleased to see me there. We ate at a restaurant off the highway. I drank water, ate salad. I was thin. She had a credit card. Installed into a room at Zen Center on Page Street with Aunti Zen down the hall, always busy. I fell into a sleep pattern, days down—up nights, in after bars closed.

One day at Zen Center I was assigned to help peel potatoes for potato salad to be served at an art opening. A large batch of potatoes must be boiled and peeled. Lou (another forgotten soul) peeled with me. We talked about Kerouac and peace in Vietnam; paraquat sprayed from helicopters on Northern California pot fields. A minion told us this was a silent work period. The spuds must be peeled hot in cold water. A right way to peel potatoes. One way to peel potatoes for salad. I felt demeaned by such dogmatic environs. I snuck down that night to raid the bread box and had a fun chat with Aunti

Zen. I asked if I could meditate in the temple instead of the zendo[1]. "No." When we prayed and bowed in the temple, I was sure I chanted wrong, mouthing words, reading phonetic chant sheet. Church. Always in doubt. The right way. Zen way.

I got tired of my routine, so I took the day to walk down Page Street from the Zen Center, where I'd stayed since being thrown out of the Treatment Center on Pine at Bush, up on Nob Hill. I had been editing copy for a small newsletter and working on the second draft of my novel. The first draft having been confiscated by the authorities in Cincinnati with my stash. I still had only one pair of desert boots. It was untitled and when I'd had it returned to me it was a jumbled mess, but I liked it better . . . THE STORY OF HOW I LOST IT AND WHAT WAS HAPPENING TO IT . . . THAT'S ANOTHER STORY. All I did was write and drink at bars; I lived off the money mother sent, and Aunti's seven dollars a day bargain at the Zen Center. Some days, I felt guilty enough to work in the kitchen, where kind people would instruct me on what to do, after I bowed in at the altar. The Zen Center itself was a center for robed figures who scurried about making important decisions while I felt meek and unimportant, making silly judgments about pages and potatoes. Walking down Page Street, I stumbled when my toe caught an uneven sidewalk, and a small white dog barked, scurrying past on a tall woman's leash. I'd worked at the Tassajara Bakery for a day. As a counterrevolutionary, I took money, but they offered me a steady job washing dishes. I declined. Later I wondered how different and relevant my life may have been had I taken that job.

Once on Market Street, I felt better, and found the

---

1   zendo—In Zen Buddhism, the *zen-dō* is a spiritual *dōjō* where *zazen* (sitting meditation) is practiced.

nice Greek restaurant the painter, who lived next door, had shown me. The painter had very wide thumbs. He gave me Johnnie Walker and green reefer while we played Go[2] and listened to jazz on the radio. He had painted the signs around the restaurant; consequently, the painter ate free. I couldn't afford to eat there often, but I came around anyway just to watch the waitress. She was loose with the way she'd talked to the painter . . . he'd say, "Honey" this, "Honey" that, etc. The painter was almost fifty and spoke a little Greek.

On this particular morning around six I had come in from a night of drinking, gone to sleep, and suspecting I had slept all day (it being light out till ten at night), saw a clock at nine, figured it to be evening, chose a stool at the long, yellow counter, and ordered dinner after hungrily checking the wine list, and decided against starting again. After finishing the souvlaki and coffee I tried unsuccessfully to walk out on the bill which came to three dollars and some change. I decided to walk to the cable car and visit the wharf, now knowing it was morning. The streets and sidewalks were crowded, noisy, moving. I passed a tall man carrying a funny looking guitar case. I watched the man. A famous rock musician with an electric guitar. A sense of importance about the day filled me. I wore tired jeans and a blue velour vest. I'd felt dirty that morning after almost walking out on the painter's friends. I rationalized that the owner of the restaurant was a gambler, played Vegas, and that had made it fair. And besides, I had not managed to walk out on the check after all. There had been a moment of embarrassment when I brushed my brown hair aside and looked away.

---

2 **Go** is an abstract strategy board game for two players in which the aim is to surround more territory than the opponent. The game was invented in China more than 2,500 years ago and is believed to be the oldest board game continuously played to the present day.

By the time I reached the Civic Center I figured out that it was Saturday. A crowd spread out on the lawn on this summer-like, spring day. Not a large group, but they were chanting. When I got closer to City Hall a fellow asked me to join the group with the petitions. They were the Rebel Worker's Party[3], circling the building with paper petitions against Proposition 13[4] which someone said would cut jobs and services. They had taped the petitions together and rolled them into a scroll which they unwound. They didn't have quite enough petitions so only two-thirds of the circle was complete. I tooted my bamboo flute which I took from the treatment center over the protestations of a staff member. The fluting sounded fine, felt good; so, I sat on a bench whistling and fluting for pigeons until the Trots offered me all the literature, then I got up, signed the petition and joined the last of the snake. By this time, nearly noon, the crowd grew to three thousand and they had megaphones and a stage. As before, in this kind of protest, I felt a sense of freedom and pleasure that came with real good organization. The song sheets were there on time. The protesters had a skit which I forgot even while I watched it, so by the end it lost meaning. When the skit petered out, I walked up the street to have an apple juice to cheer myself up.

I returned to the plaza area after chatting a bit more with some Rebel Workers, mostly workers taking the day off

---

3   Rebel Worker's Party—a loosely connected, left-wing, California, grass roots movement in the mid-70's that formed a political bloc to oppose Proposition 13. Many were participants in study groups and worker collectives. This was a time when strikes were considered feasible.

4   Proposition 13—An amendment to the California Constitution (officially named the People's Initiative to Limit Property Taxation) enacted in 1978.

for the protest. I saw someone I knew, Woodman's friend, we'd shot pool in a lesbian bar some months back before Woodman took me to Lone Pine. I chatted her up, then I walked to Powell Street and hopped the cable car.

At the wharf there were the familiar landmarks: A Cost Plus, a lot of merchants, and today, a troupe of beauties from a pageant. I looked at turquoise jewelry for a while. Nothing I wanted. Just past the fellow on the corner with the big chrome machine with all the gears that turned a penny into a curled copper disk with the Lord's Prayer for a quarter— not the same fellow I had seen doing that in New Orleans, but the same kind of machine—a magician on the wharf wore a top hat. I flashed back to New Orleans where a Hendrix lookalike played after Mardi Gras, thought of the van gone back to Harvard and my return to the streets. Those had been better times, because I'd hooked up with girlfriends and had more money in my pocket. I remembered when the magic was there inside, when I'd had more confidence, a place to stay where I was with folks of common minds. But somehow, I saw it wasn't so bad, I would write books, and later they would sell. Magazines would carry me through these times. Now the black-suited man with the top hat watched me as a group circled up. I put my cup of cola on the sidewalk, empty but for ice. The magician had five chrome rings which he put together by striking them, and when he finished, the ice in my cup exploded with a *POP!* while he passed the hat.

On the side of the drum was the lettering: *Joe V. El's Virgin Victory Band.* Joe was about five-nine and had a bushy beard, guitar, harmonica in holder, and on his shoes a tambourine with an eyebolt and cable that played the bass drum on his back. Joe, busy on the sidewalk by the water's edge, played loudly on the harp when I approached. Many years later I got the gag, "Jovial's!" On the bench next to Joe, sat a barefoot fellow who looked enough like I had when I was younger and skinnier that I was almost taken aback by the fellow's presence, somehow very large.

"All this guy wants is your money," Barefoot said.

"In my Cadillac. . ." went the song, and Joe danced around his empty guitar case, drumming the bass drum on his shoulders with the most frenetic feet since the Mardi Gras dance floor back in the dark New Orleans where I had been living off street vitamins and whiskey.

"He's just like the rest of them," Barefoot said.

There was a crash and the tinkling of green glass, a bright sound, and Barefoot spread broken glass on the sidewalk forcing long lines of people to queue up and see Joe.

"Hey! What are you doing here?" Joe asked.

"This is my spot and they're gonna have to walk around it as long as this guy keeps singing and begging for money," Barefoot said gesturing madly at Joe.

"Are you crazy?" I asked.

"I've been in nuthouses, but man, this is a free country and if I want to break glass and sell magazines in front of my bench here, there's a whole bunch of magazines here," he waved an arm at the tattered slick paper.

And sure enough, there was *Hustler* mag and a couple of Rand McNally books on America, and Barefoot, clad in ragged khaki shorts, and a torn, red T-shirt under a dirty, yellow slicker looked more troubled.

Joe stopped playing.

This stable Saturday afternoon was turning into some new kind of bizarre demonstration of civil rights for mentally ill freemen, the languid creative of San Francisco. Joe did not identify with Barefoot, but he tried to reason with him over a cigarette. They had been getting along fine, it seems, until the fellow began pestering Joe about money. I couldn't tell if Barefoot wanted a share of Joe's take, or what? The seagull on the piling flew away when the music stopped. The gull was old and blind in one eye, and Barefoot lamented his departure as he walked away from Joe.

This whole scene might fit well into my novel. Here were two comrades competing over a stretch of sidewalk, creating what was perhaps the best street theater I had ever seen. There was something dismal though. These were crippled misfits that society had left behind or outcast just as I felt cast in a role by family.

Now, Barefoot raised his voice. "This glass belongs here," he said.

"Someone could hurt themselves," said an older man.

"Hey, do you wanna see a magazine? This one has naked women! Pussies galore! Who cares about women anyway?" He said this as the girls in the beauty contest walked by in their white, summer dresses. Barefoot eyed the girls up and down, pushing himself on the afternoon.

"Listen, man, you are disturbing the peace," I said, and sat on the bench, after picking up the travel magazine.

"This is my bench, but for you I'll move the glass," he said. He surprised me by yielding, but Joe ignored Barefoot, who now seemed all the more crazy as he shouted about jumping in the bay.

Joe finished his cigarette and went back to his music, this time sounding fine and much like Zimmer[1] on this breezy afternoon. I felt self-conscious, took off my blue velour vest and laid it not on the bench beside me, but over on the turf of the one-man band, with Joe's coat, by the trash can.

Under the blue vest, I wore the lighter blue Rolls-Royce T-shirt and enjoyed being mistaken for Dick Benjy[2], the movie star. A fishing boat docked by the wharf and idled in front of where I stood, at the gate in the fence to protect passers-by from falling into the bay. I tapped with a bent silver spoon on the rail in time to the music. I picked up the spoon for a nickel in a shop on one of the crowded streets in Chinatown. I bought the spoon for no reason other than that I liked it.

Barefoot got off the bench after the fishing boat sailed.

1 Zimmer—an oblique reference to Nobel Laureate Robert Zimmerman, known popularly as Bob Dylan.

2 Dick Benjy—an obscure reference to the actor known as Richard Benjamin.

I wandered around and lost interest in the drama. I watched the people, the boats, the gulls, and the ocean. Joe and Barefoot argued again to the point where he shouted, "Stop playing or I'll jump into the bay and create such a scene you'll have to stop." Joe ignored him and kept playing. Then Barefoot gamely climbed over the railing, took off a battered yellow rain slicker, and jumped into the bay. Joe stopped playing. I left.

I saw Barefoot wrapped in his shiny slicker on a bus later that night as I made my way to a bar in the Inner Sunset. I hadn't the heart to talk to him and felt lost and empty, but imagined he was further lost.

The next morning, I waited in the hallway outside the Roshi[3]'s door where I had been promised dokusan[4]. The young monastic woman whispered in my ear, "You hear the bell, sit facing the wall . . . you get up slowly, turning as you rise, walk to the room, walk in, bow to the urn, sit facing away from Roshi, turn around after being seated, and bow to the Roshi. Don't speak until he does. Sit facing the wall." I sat facing the wall.   When I heard the bell, I walked down the hall, rose slowly, in stocking feet, turned and thought, *Why? Why am I here? Does this man know anything special? Isn't the urn just ashes, ashes of his master, the great Suzuki?*

Zen Master said, "You're my student now, it doesn't matter how you sit."   I sat facing him with my feet tucked under my knees.

"How old are you?" he asked.

"Nineteen," I said.

---

3   Roshi—a title used by a teacher who has received dharma transmission in Sōtō Zen.

4   Dokusan—work in the room! Going alone to the Master.

"You're wearing jeans. Those are too tight," he said.

"Huh?" I said.

"You're awfully young to be out here on your own. Your aunt is taking care of you. You need to either move out, get a job, or go see the psychiatrist at Mt. Zion. You're costing me too much staying here."

I gazed at this man and instantly lost all respect for him. He was another bad cop. I had hoped Zen Master could help me, now I wondered if he did anything other than watch the urn. His eyes seemed to swim around in their sockets. I left him there after saying, "I'll leave in a few days."

I packed up my few belongings in my beaten brown rucksack. On the second-to-last day of June I took the BART to the most Northern stop and began hitchhiking for Washington, DC, where I'd heard there would be a Marijuana Smoke-in on the fourth of July.

She weaved her way through the various queues, was it Wilma's daughter, Helen? The last time I'd seen her she was a teenager. A plain, flat face, vacant, eggshell blue eyes—wore no makeup, dressed in black tights, moved like a dancer, and held a hard look. Someone had told me she'd served three years in Folsom Prison. She had to be forty-three and now there was a teenage daughter in tow. We met at Customs, she took my hand, put this flat envelope in it, and placed a kiss on my cheek. "It's from your Aunti Zen, Unusually asked me to deliver it." . . . An acolyte of Unusually Tretheway?

As I stood waiting to change currency, I read my late Aunti Zen's clear handwriting: *When her mother died in 1950, Carmen took a job in Havana playing piano at a hotel nightclub. Six years later she met Louie the Lip. He was much older, married, and very smitten with Carmen. They began seeing one another, and she got pregnant just as the revolution forced both of them out of Cuba. She did not tell him she was pregnant and moved home to The Bay with her father. She lived above his restaurant, The Manhattan, on Shattuck in Berkeley for a few years, raised you there. Marty, Louie's nephew, who was sent by his Uncle Jake to find Carmen on Louie's behalf, fell in love with her at first sight. Unusually Tretheway will help you to find all this out, without too much shock. You must trust her.*

△ △ △   △ △ △

Unusually Tretheway, a tanned, Jewish, lesbian Sensei met me in Havana with her followers to help me recapture my past. She'd flown from San Francisco to Havana via Mexico

City, and rented two pink, '63 Lincoln Continentals with Cuban drivers. I had left *Pocahontas*, my yacht, in Colombia with Will and Tom.

Havana airport was small and utilitarian, lit by bare fluorescent tubes. Under-staffed it took twenty-five minutes to exchange currency. Unusually's fixer, Mr. Kosto, a compact, balding, pug-nosed sociologist posed as a photographer. In his early sixties, he spoke Spanish with a Detroit accent, and offered us two choices: we could exchange with the custodial crew in the bathroom next to the official window, have a six percent better rate, or we could go with the approved method. They took the same amount of time and were both in plain sight of the policeman with the sidearm.

△ △ △ △   △ △ △ △

Hallucination chamber. Unusually and her acolytes sit in a large peaceful yellow room around an oval table. White light filters in from tall curtained windows, quiet birds chirop outside, cars motor past and a few notes tinkle on a gut string guitar.

Back in 1978 what I didn't want to see in Cuba was where Aunti Zen came, reached out, when she got the call from the government official, who wasn't a diplomat, a USA official, something about CIA. Something about me—when the phone rang in the West Coast office it was five in the morning. A senior student took a message.

Aunti Zen was on her way to zazen[1] in the twilight zendo of Tassajara Zen Mountain Retreat Center. She walked one step at a time past the coffee bar—the skunk smell—a

---

1   Zazen—Zen meditation. The primary practice.

sweet indulgent vice. Her loose pants felt good. She didn't wear a brassiere. Her cancer was gone—the regime of garlic, carrot juice three times a day, and the San Jose based, Korean healer's supplements combined—her skin turned orange, she reeked—and now she was in remission.

After zazen she ate granola, dried apricots, raisins, almonds, and a little plain yoghurt. Then she returned the call. She hadn't known I had flown to Cuba. The official said there was a problem.

There was an ambush, and no one died—Jack blacked out at a village festival—an electric shock. He didn't have any I.D.— last she knew he had baked bread at college, bicycled cross-country, picked up the harmonica, was staying with the Merry Pranksters in Palo Alto. Now the young man had become a rockstar in crisis, not only because his sobriquet, Acid—not good in Cuba—but the Lansky family name could be a serious problem as well.

And the Welsh friend. . . Lucy. I'd never told her about Lucy, the Senator's daughter, I'd only asked a political question about the Senator and had spoken in fragments about my decision to break from college. They had eaten lunch under the wooden and tin roof two days ago, Lucy had a contact in the embassy in Washington, D.C. The two had talked before and Aunti Zen thought—the thought rushed through her like the creek ran through Tassajara Mountain after snow melted—yes, she knew I had picked up the harmonica—yes, I had stayed in Palo Alto. Less than a year had passed since the day I visited her on the way to Tassajara.

As Aunti sat at Tassajara, March 3rd, 1978, a cold morning in the zendo, a rain shower fed the creek. She smelled the dew on the platform around the zendo—smelled the green banana feet of the ino[1], heard the scraping broom, the tenzo [2]shouting at the blue jays, and the sniffling of the monk next to her as she sat facing the wall. The morning sunlight came over the ridge as she took her turn in line, walked, chanted, passed the ino, saw the pale pate, the dark robe, again smelled dank dew, and foot odor.

<u>After za</u>zen, another knock on her door from Lucy.

1   Ino—the ino is in charge of the meditation hall, or zendo, is responsible for cooperation in finding a seat.

2   Tenzo—one of the positions, and titles given in Zen Buddhism, usually limited to six or seven individuals at any given time. The tenzo is head chef, responsible for providing meals from donated and farmed goods and foods for the community.

32

Lucy said I had gambled at college. Listening to Lucy describe my erratic behavior at the college rooming house, Aunti Zen cursed Carmen for her bad choice to let me go to college back East on the bicycle and settle in without Marty and Carmen to guide me. Aunti Zen's meditation practice was the only thing that Marty had talked to her about at family Thanksgiving in Cincinnati months before when no one knew where I was. All filled in later.

I could imagine the scene: "Don't you hurt when you contort and sit? Why give yourself that pain?" Marty asked. He struggled with back problems. Carmen had told Aunti that Marty said she stank of garlic. She could not tell. She was jetlagged then. Marty sat in his Eames chair in the den, reading *Encounter Magazine*.

A HARD RAIN FELL ON HAVANA. I SAT IN THE HAVANA LIBRE HOTEL LOBBY WAITING FOR A BEER. FEBRUARY 3RD, 2017.

Usually, I sat in the front seat, this day was different. Unusually Tretheway used hypnosis to pull the story from me out of a **blacked-out** memory. I'm an alcoholic. These are memories stricken from history that no friend will ask about.

I have a Cuban photographer for a surrogate granddaughter, her name is Cloudy, she was immediately dear to me. She was openly proud to be Cuban. Her face and voice warmed me. I just met her for the first time in Cojimar yesterday with Tretheway and her followers.

She showed us her large photos of surreal city scenes from a portfolio spread on the table at a restaurant. Redspin University 2016 was carved into the wooden ceiling. "Cloudy," I asked,

"Who is your favorite rockstar?" She smelled of plumeria.

"I don't know," she said, tasted the ceviche, brushed a stray hair from her eye.

"Do you listen to American music? Do you like the blues?" I asked. "Your surreal photos could have been album covers back in the day," I said. "Redspin's my university. A shame the students would do that. Rum defiance."

"Oh, that's OK here. Kids can drink and study, carve initials on ceilings," she said.

"Cloudy, do you like the Dinkies?" I asked.

Her earrings, long and beaded, featured an evil eye. "Of course, and Zimm," she said.

"The Trolling Bones?" I asked. "Didn't they just play here?"

"Yes."

"Did you go?" I asked.

"Why ask so much about rock 'n' roll? Were you a rockstar?" she asked.

I reached for my mason jar of Longjing.

"Are you drinking dark rum?" she asked.

"It's green tea," I said, beaming and showing off the front tooth.

"You remind me of my grandfather," she said. "He was very calm and liked to tease."

We left the restaurant, walked to the shimmering sea, and next to it a skid-row boatyard, where fishermen hammered and riveted boats in the old-fashioned way. WHAT A GAIT ON THAT MAN WITH THE HAMMER WHO LOOKED AS IF HE COULD THROW AN AROLDIS[1] STYLE THREE-DIGIT FASTBALL.

Cloudy knew me right away although she never saw me. She had my dark eyes, dark hair, and her hands had

1   Albertín Aroldis Chapman de la Cruz is a Cuban-American professional baseball pitcher for the New York Yankees of Major League Baseball. He previously played in MLB for the Cincinnati Reds and Chicago Cubs and in the Cuban National Series for Holguín.

36

long straight fingers. Then we sat in her parents' living room overlooking Cojimar Bay where pelicans lounged on wood pilings. Unusually's acolytes circled Cloudy. She showed us a photograph I had taken, now displayed in a book; it depicted soldiers after the Cuban revolution printed on the ten-peso bill[2].   I am a pensive man. I squinted slightly and said nothing. This brought respect.

△ △ △ △   △ △ △ △

The pink cars rumbled to the curb. When we arrived in the next village, a day after meeting Cloudy, I promised not to tell its name, on Sunday, where the Museum exhibited old Cuban money, peso bills dating to 1896 and before, even the famous three-peso bills[3], with hemp paper and filigree, we drifted under umbrellas like explorers beneath billowed sails on great ships.

I floated through time. The mic buzzed and vibrated with electricity. No proper ground. Thankfully we were miked as the crowd grew, respectfully, drunkenness and their rowdy behavior mimicked ours. We took them up, and then. Then. Then I laid down this mighty riff. I licked the reed, I pushed my tongue up in there, striking brass, and you could not pick the melody out of the rhythm, syncopated with little crackles from the electric amp system, UNGROUNDED, REMEMBER, REMEMBER THAT, YOU NEED TO KNOW, because when the light jumped from the pole to the ground, the fight that broke out

---

2   Ten-peso bill—currency in Cuba post revolution with a special photo engraving on the backside.

3   Three-peso bill—Cuban currency depicting Che Guevara or some earlier revolutionary figure.

kicked the machine, the machine interrupted itself, and man did it fly in the face of freedom!

Δ Δ Δ Δ   Δ Δ Δ Δ

—When do I get paid? I'm a rockstar. I performed.

—You get paid when you work. You collapsed onstage.

—I performed. Your gear jammed. Your electricity jumped. I was drugged.

—You fell.

—Zapped me. Pilled me. The smoke was laced.

*—You didn't complete the show. People paid to see you. You **were** a rockstar!*

—Shit. Damn right! Your damn flim-flam crew could'a killed me. I was out four days!

—You stepped in a puddle.

—Oh, man. You've gotta at least pay me. A half a grand, a Mexico vaca?

—You were paid. Brought here, pumped up, fed, housed, transported. There's no pay left.

—No pay left? Do we perform again? I'm a rockstar.

—Not you. The rest of the band won't work with you.

—Some kind of conspiracy. Someone will. I'm the master. I play the best licks.

—You're washed up. Wasted. There were photos of you collapsed onstage. They made headlines.

—Fuck that. Fuck you.

△ △ △   △ △ △

So, drunk and in a blackout, stoned and in a distant land. Hell, I promise you I had no idea where I was until I lay in that black spot, fried by electricity and stunned. Was there a fistfight? Did I have a black eye? Were the relevant muscles damaged? Could I feel my nuts? A right-eyed man, dark patch over the left, saw this from a horse-drawn hay carriage, rushed into the crowd. I know him now because I squeezed the brake-handle on his two-wheeler forty years later, today as it rained, and we stood in the Museum where the money lay behind the glass case. On the sidewalk, Unusually leaned into my face, stood by me under a rainbow umbrella, she said, "Let go!"

And I lied. I lied about everything because before I was ten, I didn't know the truth about my family. I refused to believe it was true. I don't want to be Jack Acid, Acid Head Ve-ri-tas, great-grandnephew of Lansky the gangland crook! I don't want this mysterious past.

Let *me* describe the square. Greenery in the rain. A statue of José Martí[4]. The bust of the man with the pulled back

---

4 José Julián Martí Pérez was a Cuban poet, philosopher, essay-

hair and swept mustache. A Russian pizza place on the corner with black and white images inside. Einstein like a clown, John Lennon, Marilyn Monroe, martyrs and another face that slips into foggy memory like the town does with two horse-drawn shays passing through this Sunday. The wet street, the shoe vendor's wares covered in a black plastic tarp, and men lingering in creased trousers, smoking cigarettes, drinking long-necked Corolanas, and handling tall bottles of light Cuban rum. The vendors stood above the street and sidewalk in a covered portico that stretched the length of the building. Could it have been Bernal, Mexico in a bad Western movie from the Spaghetti period? Or, like a really awful parody of the serene, adobe village of Santa Fe, New Mexico, circa 1978? Inside the open area behind the pillars and the portico—glance again, it got away fast—inside, inside people drank, shouted as the cockfight ended. The smoke, thick, intense and full of rollicks, the rollicks of the sidling kind, I DON'T WANT TO ANNOUNCE IT, BUT THIS IS THE MOMENT THAT CASCADES FULL FRONTAL MEMORY. My story was set in that open area. After a cockfight or nearly during, they brought on this kid with a harmonica, wearing tight pants, full of piss, a lot of vinegar in his veins. Did they know he would break down mid-set as they shot, as they lit the scene using the derricks of a great film crew? It was the electricity, not the music! A pole, a pole jumped, and he went down, scorched to his knees. His legs now shorter or was he bent, photo-jammed?

So, he came to in the back of a hay wagon. A long way from there, well a farm seven kilometers away. The next day he…

---

ist, journalist, translator, professor, and publisher, who is considered a Cuban national hero because of his role in the liberation of his country.

∆ ∆ ∆ ∆   ∆ ∆ ∆ ∆

Unusually Tretheway instructed me to read *Havana Nocturne* as we sat together in the back seat. I read about Mom as Louis Lansky's Cuban mistress. He met her in 1955, fell in love in 1956 and left her when revolution came. Carmen had olive-toned skin, was not too tall, her hair in loose black curls, she had a confident stride, good balance, was soft-spoken, had fine hands, a jazz piano player, she had curves and breasts that didn't need a bra, a fine lambent hair on her arms, with knees and toes shaped like a sculpture, cat-eye glasses. . . . I was told Mother had Greek heritage. Louis Lansky. . . Jewish Mafia in 1940s and 50s Cuba. . . known to me as my grandfather, Lou, my real father?

I met him at eight years old when, with his wife, Grace, Lou visited our family in Cincinnati. He was known in mob circles as Louie the Lip. I remembered the pencil-thin mustache coupled with a quick mouth. It worked a smelly Cuban.

Lou's nephew, Marty, was my "dad," a man who claimed Carmen was my mom. When questions of my parentage came up when I was young, Marty stated, and I thought he kidded, "We know your mother." He never teased about Will, my brother, Marty's "first" son. Will had the keys to the cabinet where we kept photo archives. I had one photo of Lou in my collection. In postwar Ohio, all brothers were the same age, and Will and I grew up under the same roof, though he lorded over me his first status. But I was always bigger. No doubt I was weaned before he held the tit. Marty favored Will, and pressed me, like a delicate flower in a thick book. Teased me. Pushed me to learn to write. Marty wanted a girl.

△ △ △ △   △ △ △ △

The red-winged blackbird sat on the tail of the desiccated Cessna[5]. He moved his tail up and down—said a chit-chi-chit-a-whooeedidit-his throat bulged and he looked about the

field. Him the only life that saw the yellow and white airplane.

The years had passed—now it was a broken-winged Orphan Plane. The airport

left fifteen years ago.

I once sat in its backseat a flask of dark rum held tightly in my left hand. The redwing heard the metal creak as wind swept through the empty steel vessel. There were reasons to escape the USA for Cuba in the early 70s; these could have made a treatise— a manifesto—anti-Vietnam War—pro-commie-Hemingway Sympatico's. The excuses were coupled with fruit, rum, and Mollies[6]. I did not remember much. Looking down at the blue water, rippled with white caps—a day of fainting in and out of consciousness.

When I saw the plane in the Mayabeque Province of Cuba near Güines, fifty kilometers southeast of Havana, next to the Mayabeque River, I shit my pants. I sat next to Unusually Tretheway in the back of the pink car. After all, I had not remembered my Cuban foray—life included hitchhiking,

---

5   Cessna—An American general aircraft company known for small single engine planes.

6   Mollies—the pure crystal or powder form of the drug MDMA known in pill form as ecstasy.

smoking pot, playing benefits until I felt passively numb, and then I was propped on a stage with a microphone, surrounded by electricity—great sparking tube amplifiers—and holding the metal and wooden teeth in front of my mouth against the mic—breathing and shaping my electrified tongue—vibrations—guitars all around, surrounded by singers—their black mouth holes against chrome screens—and sound—loud, screaming sound.

They'd expected me to tuck my tall body behind the twin pilots—next to a sweet-smelling Gwendolyn—someone I knew only as a pale body close at hand. The hitchhiking had terminated into touring with musicians—lounging in white leather upholstered Cadillacs—I'd heard the others whisper in numbers about me and reserved the thought—*what anyone else thinks of me is none of my business*—and I drank the rum—played the metal teeth—became mighty Jack—Jack Acid, the harpist. The tooth harp. And the redwings came and went in this cow pasture where the yellow and white Cessna stayed to rest. It had served the rock 'n' roll state. The international musician's unions— the comrades of blues cadres. They had done what they had done.

△ △   △ △

Here's Pistolero Peter with his tip o' the hat to Hemingway on Cuba Libre, Marx and Engels Radio:
                              Pistolero   Pete,   the pelican, saw Jack and Unusually climb off the bus by Plastic Stone Beach. A shark had just come in aboard the Pilar. The fish was enough for sixty people, the cartilage could be sold for the cure, and the fins, well, fins were dried then packaged. Pistolero cared only for the guts of the shark. He would eat well and try not to share. "Your beak'll hold more than your belly can," the mockers mocked. The revolutionary principle Pete taught—"You can only eat so much at one meal. Or, don't bogart!"   Emily,   Pete's grand pelican daughter—a hatchling four years ago, liked to eat her fill but leave her bill empty. Pete tried to teach her otherwise. She said, "Hola! Granpa, que pasa—? May I use your plastic arts again today?" Emily knew that pelicans and other birds could not digest plastic. If they ate it, it could not pass, it would fill their stomachs and they would starve, blocked by plastic, unable to digest food. Tourists approached quietly holding glass, AI spyglasses, entranced by their contempt for the garbage, smell, and desiccation of Plastic Stone Beach. There was a particular stance, the lean, the fingers extended. Jack wanted to document the garbage plastic on the beach. The bulldozer, hidden away for years didn't interest him. He wanted the womyn, Unusually's acolytes, to stoop and pick up plastic by hand, their feet in dirt. In Cabo San Lucas, Baja California, Mexico the powerful yellow bulldozers were mounted on pedestals to honor their contribution to the cleansing of the beaches; here, they hid like the Orphan Plane, crumpled, rusted, in tall grass.

The womyn walked to the shed where fishermen cleaned the shark. They documented the run-down boatyard and watched the workmen, going about their day in the heat.

Alonso, a black Cuban of Cojimar owned a hammer. He spent the day drinking rum and pounding nails into milled planks. His job was to keep the docks from slipping and falling into the bay. Base camp for the fishermen changed little day-to-day. The chain-link fence and the armed guard made that stick. Alonso didn't speak to the guard except when leaving in the morning—he hammered during the day and night. And he drank the dark rum, while he tossed the shark's entrails on the beach for Pete, Emily, and the other circling, gray, and white birds.

Cloudy listened to Cuba-Libre, Marx and Engels Radio on ear buds as she walked in Vedado past the National

Ballet to meet Pepé at the Monument to John Lennon. After a sunny, muffled bit of static she heard the bubbly host speak:

Thanks for listening to Cuba-Libre, Marx and Engels Radio. WE play literary snippets from the Palo Alto of the Americas. That was Pistolero Peter the surrealists' plausticity! Next a bit of JA and I'm not talking Junior Achievement. This goes out to Cloudy, chronicling an Acid fueled journey, written and performed by Steven Lansky from 1977.

We were three, Woodman, Dick and me, heading down the night highway out of Garberville, California in Mendocino County, the United States' marijuana growing capital. A couple of hours earlier we got the tour from a bushy-bearded, tall, thirty-year-old hippie with a stacked, purple backpack full of Sinsemilla, packed carefully and ready for distribution. Four of the downtown buildings were burned down shells, a carbon and creosote reminder of the struggle. "The hippies own the town," said our new friend. "You can go into any of the three realty offices here and put down money on land and get a loan to grow. Jimmy Carter and the Feds are looking the other way, and so is Governor Brown. This is business." We offered him a ride east in Dick's orange VW microbus, but he said, "I'm bound for Oregon." But not before he gave us a fat ounce, "Just a taste from someone who cares," he said.

Woodman tugged at his big red beard, turned his sunburnt face to show the diamond stud in his left ear. "We'll go to Flagstaff, work for the Forest Service, save a few grand and come back. We'll be farmers." None of us disagreed, I rolled a fatty, Dick coughed her through the gears, and we puttered east. After a while we all had a good buzz and I pulled out a harmonica and went into a musical dense haze. Improvising, wailing, bending, and pumping chords, sound filled the narrow space.

"A hitchhiker!" said Dick. He pulled the van to the shoulder. The man was short, obviously Hispanic, a dark bowl of shaggy straight hair framed his round face. He had one of those big

packs, and he slid the door back smoothly, climbed in as I shifted rhythms.

"Hey, cool music, man," he said, and then introduced himself. HERE'S WHERE THE STORY TAKES A LITTLE LEAP.

He either said, "Carlos," or "Santana," just one word, but I can't remember which one.

"Woodman," said Woodman, "Dick's driving, and this is Jack," he said. And Carlos smelled the weed with his wide nostrils flaring. "Some of mine?" he asked. I nodded while still wailing, and the others followed. Carlos pulled out an elaborate hand-carved, dark wooden bowl in the shape of a magic dragon, filled it with bud, and we got even higher. I paused in the music long enough to toke. Then I was back to the harp and the sound of the motor, the reeds and the smell of grass floated us over the road.

"Where ya headed?" asked Woodman.

THE STORY LEAPS AGAIN HERE.

Carlos either said, "Reno," or "Tahoe," and, "Going picking up a semi-tractor trailer to bring to Mendocino ta load with the harvest.

*D*istribute the whole West Coast. Cooperative business, man," he said.

I wondered why one of the worlds' rock 'n' roll gods was moonlighting in marijuana but somehow in the haze and the blues, it made a sense all of its own. And soon we dropped the short Latin backpacker out onto the highway as we sped toward our destinies in Lone Pine.

Thanks for listening to Cuba-Libre, Marx and Engels Radio. WE play literary snippets from the Palo Verde of the Americas. That was Carlos the Calipsychedelia! It went out to Cloudy, chronicling adventures of JA, and I don't mean Junior Achievement, written and performed by Steven Lansky. This is DJ Libre, himself.

Pepé, a tall musician, with a dark beard, sat next to Lennon's bronze on the bench waiting for Cloudy. Unusually Tretheway stood by the Chinese built tour bus and rang her meditation bell to signal the end of the visit at John Lennon Park. I finished up my sketch, and as Cloudy arrived, with her dancer's body, she stood on her toes to kiss Pepé's lips. The view of her backside, callipygian and magnificent sent a kundalini ripple up my spine.

△ △ △ △   △ △ △ △

We sat with Unusually Tretheway. I saw the candles on the side table in the parlor of Santa Bridgida Convent and thought about the two silver candlesticks on the dining room table where I grew up in Ohio. One crinkled and twisted at the thinner part of the stem. Both silver, ornate design, and otherwise identical with blue felt on the bottoms. A voice sang a Spanish folksong with a guitar. I thought of Mommy, Carmen. Wondered who gave her those lovely candlesticks and how one got twisted and why she kept the pair on display in the dining room because the damage? Were they handed down by her mother? Her father? From Greece—Thessaloniki? Or, Russian? From Ukraine? Could the moment here with the lilting Spanish voice while we sat in the salon in Habana Vieja be a clue to the candlesticks' damage?

The perfume of the room—a light sprig of mint, perhaps. Here now with an old friend of Aunti Zen, yeah Cuba, touring with twenty womyn, aging angst at the memory of candlesticks. Were there silver smiths or sliver importers, pirates of the Caribbean who gave or sold them to Lou or Grace? Passed down to Carmen? Did Lou twist one of them in a fit? Jealous rage? The fact of these silver candlesticks, black and silver elegance, blue felt bottoms, the twisted one kept side-by-side with the good one put me in mind of Mom and Aunti Zen. Two sisters. One flawed. One aged gracefully. Where are the candlesticks? One twisted in a jealous rage.

I'm not looking at them now. Because they were a memory. I saw them. Their weight in my hands as they became lighter while I grew older and my hands got bigger. I'm not telling you what I'm not looking at because you might see through to the moment of jealous rage—unremembered—unhinged—and angry. Anger held a knot between my shoulder blades. An instrument of destruction in the jealousy— jealous rage that damaged more than smoke or twisting.

I wasn't looking at drunken, red-faced, angry Marty breaking a plate on his birthday—dropping special, ceramic platter with chocolate, cheesecake falling, spilling, leaving Carmen to clean up sticky, brown and yellow, cream cheese, and egg. Marty headed out alone to drive. She worried at home with her boys as the light dimmed in the staggered French windows.

Was it twisted by drunken Lou when his nephew, Marty, told Lou he bought a motorcycle? They drank, until Lou offered to buy it? Young Marty planned to ride cross-country from Boston to Portland, Oregon after he ceremoniously graduated from Harvard in '49. I wasn't looking at that motorcycle, but it could've been the moment. The argument that ended with his aunt Grace, Lou's wife, taking his side.

And this, this could have originated the twisted candlestick and the twenty-something man leaving with saddlebags packed, roaring the green, army motorcycle, his throat wrapped in a scarf, leather jacket zipped. When Marty never returned from the left coast with Carmen and three sons.

△ △ △   △ △ △

Seated on a bench in John Lennon Park, I sketched a panel ice-cream truck[1] that a man restored from forty years before. Plastic and tape covered where a window had been. The man was away at a second-hand store while I sketched. On Pod an electrified harmonica beat a steady, punchy, honking rhythm. I remembered walking as a teenager, meeting John here with Mickey. They met me off the bus. I didn't remember the Cessna, or the accident. I just knew these two met me at the edge of Havana. The year for me was 1978, for them 1963.

△ △   △ △   △ △

A stairway into a grotto.

Large unfinished stone sculptures of porous igneous rock.

A brown eyed boy playing by himself.

Drilling in the street at a distance.

Hydrotherapy[2] in a large state-run facility.

Water cascading into a deep tub.

<u>Absolute freedom</u> from self-consciousness about nakedness.

1   Small delivery van with painted sign on the side. Term coined circa 1910.

2   Hydrotherapy—or hydropathy and water cure, a medical practice in state run psychiatric hospitals that involved immersion in deep baths with fast running water. Also practiced recreationally with counter-culture drugs. Hot tubs.

Red beehives.

A mild social discontent.

Addiction to marijuana.

Social welfare as a government policy and how the drug industry controls it.

A dead man in the bed next to mine.

I awoke in a facility. The bed had steel tubes. Last night they moved me to this room from the lockup. I pissed the floor in the lockup. Now I don't remember if they let me shower after pissing the room. I don't remember if I peed on myself. I know I was barefoot. Was this before or after the hydrotherapy? I think after. My foot had healed. I was ready to go. I slept peacefully for the first time in days.

The man in the bed next to mine coughed through the night. In the morning he was still. I don't remember who checked on him. Did I find him dead? Did a nurse, or aide? Was this still a detention facility? How could a man that old be detained here?

They came for the body. I remember vaguely some scurrying around. THIS IS NOT AUTOMATIC WRITING. I felt a mild social discontent. This addiction to marijuana was not managed by the orange pills they gave me.

A dead man in the bed next to mine.

I remember an absolute freedom from self-consciousness about nakedness during the hydrotherapy. I don't remember the cause for the tile room. It was a fabulously appointed state-run facility. Outside in the yard there were large unfinished stone sculptures of porous igneous rock, a stairway into a grotto and a brown-eyed boy playing by himself.

I heard drilling. I thought we were in the country. The boy ran from red beehives into a marsh nearby. His feet on the pavement were thumps on my disturbed, worried mind. Had they taken the corpse away and let me sit outside to play harmonica? I remember a room with a piano. Don't know which happened first. Where was I when they returned my backpack? Where was I when I looked at my journal? The green walls. I had left the pack on a street corner when I took the drive in the Rolls-Royce.

Now, a dead man next to me. A gaunt man with wrinkles. Horribly disturbed. No money. Self-imposed exile. When I packed my bag, I took the blanket from that room. Spring Grove, Maryland stitched tag on the gray blue striped wool. I took a white shirt.

They returned my broken shoes.

There had been a stop in jail. Is this fact or fiction? No way to tell. Whispering. Pinch me awake.

Describe the dead man, physically.
How old was I?
Tell about the Rolls-Royce and the mnemonic and license plate.

Do you have a cigarette?

Can you describe the last dead body you have seen?

I made a decision a long time ago not to see dead bodies.

Moments that are painful or rude to enter, he says about asking questions. Journalists and writers can be cruel.

Writing about it and avoiding the actuality. Explore avoidance.

Empathy and theatre. Shadows.

It could be a movie.

Burlap sacks of unripe fruit. Mangos, bananas, cocoanuts, and passion fruits on the floor of the plane. The sacks were damp as if mushrooms were going to grow in them later. I didn't want to be there. Sick of flying in small planes, full of fear, I knew only to take Xanax and red wine. The flight from Big Pine Key, Florida to Santiago de Cuba had to be merciful. Short enough that I passed out for it, but on either end the waking came hard. The fruit kept it seemingly legal. If we were caught, I was a hitchhiker.

No US Passport could fly out of Cuba to the US during the embargo.

The orphan plane. Back seat for me.

I saw the plane's shadow move faster over the mottled green farms.

The aviator glasses rolled off my face. When I leaned against a burlap covered cocoanut, I felt the glass splinter, but somehow the luck kept it from leaving the teardrop frame. I made a decision long ago not to see dead bodies.

Δ Δ   Δ Δ   Δ Δ

We walked, John's long legs, Mickey[3] in his silk white shirt. I held two Marine Bands[4] in one hand, a third in a shirt pocket. Right now, the harp in my ears substituted for the money. No need for money, just pills and the electricity. I had the green Astatic Bullet mic in a purple sock that hung from my belt. The three of us stopped in this park. Not yet named John Lennon Park. We made it famous as the two of them sang, and I harmed. I riffed four riffs that no one ever heard. When they asked how to play them, well, gifted them. One called: *Love Me Too*, a second: *Please Please Leigh*, a third,

*P*iddley Patty, and a fourth *From Me To Who*. Cuba time warp interfyced John and

Mickey, got my licks from the 70s, snuck them back to the 60s using the Arcturian tech. We had no electricity, so it wasn't a concert, just three lads trying to get with two runaway lanky girls. One of the girls left with Mickey, the other sat next to us and put her tongue in my ear. John ran after an ice cream truck.

———————————

3   Mickey—a reference to the lead singer in a British rock 'n' roll band referred to later in the text as the Trolling Bones.

4   Marine Band—a model of Hohner ten-hole diatonic harmonica. Most widely available and cost effective.

△ △ △ △   △ △ △ △

After the electric accident and the ride in the hay wagon—I made my helpers give me directions to the city. I asked and shouted how I was important as my name was *Acid*. There was a club in New York City with my name, *Lansky's*, and I knew Lucy, the New York Senator's daughter. The thin man with the golden skin, and eye-patch, who had taken me in the two-wheeled horse-cart, listened—then he hid me. In Cuba the thing to do with a mysterious person out of NYC was hide him.

The smell of hay and horse manure filled my nose as I reached a hand to find an electric light switch by the hewn wooden door. The shadow receded, the Arabian rustled, and I felt a trickle of sweat on the inside of my shirt. Barefoot. Shoes stolen? Did I doff them when I played the harm? I played barefoot. The dirt floor felt good, the hay stuck between my toes. I remember One-Eye brought me carrots and oranges all the way from China. I washed them down with rum and fed orange carrots to Buddy the Arabian horse.

One afternoon—on the second or third day, One-Eye gave me a cold bottle of beer. He asked me if I could hit a baseball? I told him I wasn't sure. The beer was yeasty and strong. It stopped the tremor in my wrist. I had three pills of MDMA[1] left in the sewn pocket of my khakis. We called it X.

I walked and hitched a ride to Havana.

She carried a Guatemalan purse. Hand-woven in muted colors with an orange highlight that stood out both because of the color, and the jagged triangular line it drew around the outside girth of the bag. Large, with long handles—it hung on her shoulder.

The back of her tight black shirt was open, crisscrossed with a netlike effect— scooped in front. A necklace with a red stone and two golden crystals were set together.

A hammered gold fan spread on her white chest. Her eyes and tits both held allure. The blue of her eyes a shade unlike the cerulean sea—more sky—so pale, shimmered in the interior of the café.

I sat alone within the outer columns, down one step from the red and white checked tile floor, around the perimeter. Six pillars wrapped in rope below a rail confined ten rectangular tables, surrounded by straight-backed, wooden chairs, blue on blue striped cushions, highlighted yellow. Like a sculpture, the rope mirrored a central courtyard— lower, but, down then up again for the Cuban girl in the open-backed blouse. A tacky swordfish hung next to the TV on the far,

---

1   MDMA—The pill form of Mollies, a street drug known as Ecstasy.

yellow wall. Cubans smoked cigars, drank from long-necked, brown bottles, their eyes flashed dark intent. The walls had French windows, wooden framed, vertical panes of reflective glass.

Sitting for sixteen-hour days at Restaurant Cafeteria, I smoked roll-ups, and drank beer. Good and drunk, I stammered, played harp, and lived on the street in the blackout. Time then telescoped and compressed, elastic as the plasticity that the chemicals caused my brain to fluctuate in and out of the real. The space bristled with familiarity. Around the corner and down the alley to San Francisco Square that would someday host a bronze statue to me, *the friendly*: homeless man who fed the cats.

The server's shape—an hourglass and her delightful, mischievous grin, like young Radha. You could see her with your third eye, eating butter. The ridge of her shoulders looked so calm, so reasoned, a necessary refuge for a child in a storm. I asked her help and trusted she could navigate the menu—The lilt in her voice turned me into cornmeal mush—my staple breakfast. She raised her eyebrows listening—brought polenta, said words and scribbled on her hand or a pad—it depended on how much a tip she required in her mild treachery. I called her Gwendolyn for a reason, but I don't remember what it was. She called me Jack. The light in her eyes—a fiery mist—she **knew duende**[2].

The other customers in the café talked of the rock show they had seen in the theatre two blocks away. The musicians came to unwind. She served ceramic mugs to the elders, plastic and paper cups to younger patrons; her ethos of ecology tied to the thought patterns of the larger society. She arched her white

---

2   Duende—Spanish term for a heightened state of emotion, passion, expression, and authenticity. The term comes from folklore and has been connected with flamenco.

neck for a bigger tip. I endured that because I had a white, Panama hat.

A bicycle slid past the window—the overhead fan beat so slowly it was hard to believe it turned. San Francisco Square and the fountain flowed without water, a short walk away.

△ △ △ △   △ △ △ △

This time, Unusually Tretheway's bus waited, idled, my blackout revealed in the burdensome space of the twenty-five-minute pencil sketch. A bronze of young John sat on a wooden, park bench on the other side of the park. The tour guide explained that a guard sat to watch over John's wire-rimmed glasses. Otherwise people stole them. I saw neither the glasses, the guard, nor a reflection, elusive as the blackout, mysteries in the flow.

At the next stop we bought ice cream. The dream fugue fractured. Somehow without a new memory I had sex with the lanky girl, spent the better part of four days and nights after the Mollies. Then I stood in the multi-level complex with the angry Cuban vendors who did not serve me. The remembered fragment that I stripped off my clothes, shouted, was wrestled into a strait jacket, and more blackout until hours then foggy memory having dinner with Aunti Zen, Tom, and the Ambassador. In the here and now, I bought ice cream sandwiches for Unusually and her acolytes.

Decades later in the restaurant where I had dined with the Ambassador, Phil

Spivey, the poker star, played piano, with a jazz trio, and his little ears. Soni Mitchell and a man sat at a table behind Tretheway. We sang along. After she finished her wine, her octogenarian eyes gracing her way past us to the door, Mitchell said, "You sound good." Phil relaxed as he tickled the eighty-eights instead of flopping the fifty-twos. Dark wood, white linen, fluted goblets, and a starched-suited waitress served us. But now as I sipped San Pellegrino, and sucked meat off the bone of a rabbit, the knuckles of its spine yielding tasty marrow, I remembered that Aunti Zen had never met me in Havana.

She had convinced Marty and Carmen to come and bring Tom. The three of them and the U.S. Ambassador had treated me to a dinner that came with:

—*Do you know you cannot do this forever? Your mind and body will give out.*

—You're kidding. I can go on like this. Maybe a few years I'll have to pull back a little. I can keep it.

—Come home with us to Cincinnati. See a doctor.

—Cuban medicine.

—Cuban medicine is more wine and rum.

—Champagne for me. The best.

—No more champagne. We'll cut the purse strings.

—You won't. It won't matter.

—We will. Then you're naked again.

—Excuse me.

I stalked to the restroom, scored a beer on the way from a waiter's silver tray—hit you later—and found two more pills in the lining of my coat. Chewed them down with the beer, took a piss, returned to the table. The buzz came in slow but not easy. The stiff leather, cowboy boots hurt my feet. Heels were too big, too high, even for sitting on that smelly overstuffed chair. The white coats and black ties looked like little robot birds, carrying their shitty trays.

Δ Δ Δ   Δ Δ Δ

The light in the inner court loved the trees, plants, and stuffed birds, expressions of Santeria.

Full after a breakfast of papaya, almonds, pistachios, mango juice, and warm milk poured over the nuts and fruit I sipped Longjing brewed in the jar with agua caliente de sister Mary Adelle at Convent Santa Bridgida. In Unusually Tretheway's care right now—WE KEPT THE LAMP LIT, released bits of our overexposed photos and scribbles. The fish tank supported a pair of piranhas, and was topped by a sculpture of a shark, reminding us that predatory people swam amongst as if we're food for the masses.

A shout, repeated, "Seven, number seven, seven, seven!" A man in a brown Franciscan robe helped the vested waiter, carried round trays, one at a time and wiped tables with a gray and white rag—it was difficult to tell if the two men brought or took away food, plates, bowls, cutlery that clinked, and jangled amid the twitter of songbirds loose, and flying in and among the chairs, hats, ham and eggs, tables, and beakers.

The odor of diesel and sound of a truck engine, then the hiss of brakes released pressure as did the familiar gaze, nod, and conspiratorial wink from one of two Englishmen I'd seen the night before at a four table Paladar[1] where the food had been devilishly cold and took a long time to come from the window of the kitchen to the next room. Last night the kitsch kept company with the tall man in a black baker's hat, who sprinted up and down the stairs—tried to catch his moustache, but no, it ran faster, faster, faster. This morning, my watered-down, pineapple orange juice in a tall, sweaty, fluted goblet flared at

---

1   Paladar—small restaurant run by self-employers. Usually in a house or residence.

the rim was just ice, and a few elusive drops—it dripped on my shorts—the last part of a drink hard to pull from such a glass. In a fight with the family, it was easy to take the dregs. Even though I was accustomed to cream.

I remembered pain and punishment. When I sat with teacher. Teacher told me. Teacher don't tell me, I thought. What was this voice? Me? Did remembrance of small children stir it? When Grandmother sat at the table, she told me not to whistle like he did.
He was Grandfather Lou. As if Dad were nothing. Nothing. Nothing, I remember a voice.

"Cheated." They touched hands, poking, gestured, with comic conspiratorial smiles.

"You—seven-thirty. Dinner." Like Grandmother Grace paused as Louie, Louie, she called him, "Louie, can you whistle Dixie?" And they had playing cards in their man and woman hands. Hands fanned out the red backed Bicycle cards—she laid them on the table—he began to chew on his cigar, mouth worked under the moist lips, a pencil thin moustache lined evenly over his teeth, yellow and stained. The whistle began….

Only a little I remember those days in Cuba. I know now we were there for the holidays but called it Costa Rica because they didn't want me to know Grandfather was half-brother to LANSKY, the man whose name blazed across a paperback in white capital letters—I photographed him reading. I remembered buying the paperback biography in the drugstore, in Cincinnati where I rode my bicycle to Pete's News to buy bubble gum. I saw our name and asked them about it. I watched Lou read but never got a clear answer. Mom didn't like Cuba. And the photo of Lou, he smoked, it's there somewhere.

Unfortunately, the Merry Pranksters Cannot Be Trusted.

A few years ago, after Marty died, I went through his dusty vinyl collection. He owned a lot of classical, and five early Yoan Taez albums, including two copies of #5, a mist cloaked tree on one with a warped cover, both with scratches on "Here but for Fortune," but what struck gold was the New York Bro Musica Ensemble. I found a familiar musician from over thirty years back when I lived in Palo Alto at eighteen. Dad's scrawl dated 1962, Harvard. He'd seen them. Her name: Martha Block. She had become my mentor.

Circa 1976: We were in Bryant Street House in the yellow, space-time, bus stop kitchen. "My friend, Gary, the writer, he teaches at Foothill Junior College," Wilma said. "You could meet him."

"I'd like that," I said, pushing back my glasses against a thin nose.

Gary had published *Divine Rightly's Trip* in *The Last Mole Earth Catalog*. From the first time I'd read this novel as marginalia, serialized page-by-page, it intrigued me. I became a student of Gary's while I taught kindergarten at a Quaker school for privileged kids. Later I would teach at Redspin, the alma mater of Ed MacMahan[1] and Ken Gabbs[2] (Kesey's right-hand man). Teaching undergrads about homelessness included a critical study of this *Trip*.

As an idealist most of my life, I sought, and gave, guidance. I still spend a lot of time trying to forget Wilma,

---

1   Ed MacMahan—a clumsy misspelling of McClanahan, a Lexington, Kentucky based author with ties to the Merry Pranksters.

2   Ken Gabbs—a corruption of the name Ken Babbs, an Oregon based novelist and amateur trombone player who was known to affiliate with some of the Merry Pranksters.

and the redwood house we lived in, a woman and a place out of literature, literally, as the home had been Ed MacMahan's, and the site of the Free University[3] in the 1960s. A design for living low, the full-length, smelly porch had hanging begonias, fleas, in an overstuffed couch, ashtrays, and empty wine jugs. The common rooms were occupied by Roy Webern's[4] quixotic psyche-shaved paintings, and another one's strange noise-making sculptures. MacMahan described the redwood two-story, where the roof tilted, in his book *Famous People Who Have Known*. Roy, dubbed: "Secretary of the Interior" by Kesey painted *Further*[5], lived in a tiny camper parked in our driveway and smoked weed with Wilma—her inspired sobriquet, "Generally Famished" as she appeared in Tom Wolfe's *Electric Kool-Aid Acid Test*, hungry, pregnant, and scribbling scores to settle. She had two kids with different fathers. (Helen, the older kid, was now an acolyte of Tretheway's.) Wilma became a lawyer, but in the mid-seventies worked as a paralegal, had earned an ABD in philosophy, and at forty-years-old plied me—at eighteen—with Daniels, Wild Turkey and Method Acting[6].

---

3   Free University—it's hard to tell what really happened here, suffice it to say people learned, enjoyed each other, and taught, and nobody got caught, or seriously hurt, and there were few successful administrators.

4   Roy Webern—an international othering of Roy Sebern, an artist, Merry Prankster, and friend. At one point he repainted a brightly colored canvas olive green to make a green rectangle that balanced at least six other green rectangles in a backyard. These included a grass roof, a fence, a blind, the side of a shed, a lawn, and who knows what else. Roy had a simple way of weaving color, space, and concept.

5   Further—also spelled Furthur, the Magic Bus driven by Neal Cassady. A great social experiment in mind-altering, freedom sharing transport, this vehicle left an intrepid mark on the universe.

6   Method—a school of acting based on Uta Hagen's techniques. Refer to Stanislavsky for further insight into this emotional

In Gary's third lesson we heard Martha Block sing.

Gary said, "She's the **real** teacher," after a cappella *Makin' Childer by Shteam*[7]. This Irish ballad divulged how modernity screwed up screwing. As Gary took a leak in the alley later that night behind an ass smelly dumpster, the kind that burns your eyes, he said, "If I were a younger man, I might get with her."

At fifty, Martha's eyes played younger. The gray swirl of them sent my insides adrift. Con-artist musician eyes, older spirit-guide eyes, almost stolen from an Alias I met six months earlier on the street outside a San Francisco Laundromat.

Martha offered me a banjo lesson when we were having beers at the pub.

A week later I sat next to her on her couch. We touched at the hip while she placed her waxy hands on my fingers, showed me how to hold the instrument, fret as you elbowed the hard, round drum into your belly to shape hollow tones, and how to flick the strings. "Claw-hammer style," she said. "Hold your index and middle fingers stiff. We'll start with two or three fingers."

She left me frailing on the couch.

When she returned the conversation shifted. Frustrated with banjo, she smelled of clover, white musk, and opium powder. She served white wine.

At our Bryant Street swarp[8], we heard two fresh Wilber identification.

7   *Making Children by Steam*—an Irish ballad about Daniel O'Connell and the industrialization of swyving.

8   Swarp—a term coined in Appalachia where Twain met Wikipedia. Another word for a musical, literary gathering or party. Not in parlance anymore. Until after the pandemic, anyway.

stories[9], that weren't fresher than Johnny Popp's[10]; he read us a story about driving while masturbating. His brother wore a homemade orange denim jump suit, and in the kitchen, the un-mechanized, space-time bus stop, pitched his yurt-for-sale yarn style. The one he built by hand on public property in a redwood glade near La Honda behind Kesey's place.

Martha invited me to a workshop. At the time, *the German* arrived on the scene, a fellow with slick black hair who visited her in the afternoons. He stank of harsh cologne. By then, comfortable with her, you might say *in her spell*, I ate beets and sweet potatoes she cooked in her microwave then served with fresh butter and yoghurt. Rooted, you may say. Hansel to her wicked intentions. She had the microwave on a free trial with no intention of keeping it. The funny cigarette. Then she inflated her purple hat…however you do that. *The German* picked up his clothes in a green laundry bag. His sharp blue-gray eyes found mine, and his face registered relief and exhaustion. He looked to be in his thirties. They broke up.

Speaking of the workshop, she would explain, "It's based on the work of Bandler and Grinder, psychologists who invented this *method*. Gary will be there." I heard this, and while fascinated with the words, the way she shaped the words fretted her lips more even than what she said. *Would the German, would he be there, too?* I sang.

She said, "No."

Sitting on the couch, side-by-side, touching at the hip, banjo cradled, fingers plucking, fretting, moving over to her hair, brushing it away from her face, then kissing.

The banjo lesson progressed.

A week later, we rendezvoused at an outdoor wedding

---

9 Wilber stories—an intentional misspelling of Wilgus.

10 Johnny Popp—A legendary writer, farmer, and carpenter from Oregon.

one night in a dust-fragrant grove of Eucalyptus where she was the hired attraction. I rode there on THE BLUE RACING BICYCLE. Martha sang a cappella, *Nine Times a Night,* a song played on KFAT Radio from Gilroy, the garlic capital of the world. She plied her Celtic harp when her voice required accompaniment, pulling strings with waxy, rangy fingers.

Another time we drove with her harp in the back of my pickup truck to a country fair in Marin under a clear blue sky. The valley smelled of salt sea as we walked barefoot among the hippies, the acoustic music sweet, a background susurrus from the Pacific, while they danced. I dressed in a puffy, itchy costume *the German* had left behind, some sort of Renaissance Festival garb. In a flowing brown skirt, and on crutches, Martha complained that her cast chafed her crotch.

Six days later the lutenist, Julian Dream, performed at Foothill Junior College, Martha took me backstage after the show. We drank mead. He gushed over her, shook my hand and said, "Any friend of Martha's is good to know." I drove home in the pickup truck the morning after Julian's concert. The garden gate open, the window on my cottage door broken, Macho, the dog, staggering, bewildered and THE BLUE BICYCLE GONE stolen from the bathroom. The six hundred-dollar bills stashed in the plastic lid of a spray paint can undisturbed. The blue Folli[11], worth more than the truck, ridden from Cincinnati to Cambridge by way of Ann Arbor and Toronto, across the Eastern states into Ontario the summer after, and in the summer of 1975 across Wyoming, over the continental divide. No one at the commune, (I had moved from Bryant Street to East Palo Alto, with Wilma, and some others, including seven chickens, one duck, a goat, and thirteen bunnies) no one had heard the break-in. Macho had not barked.

---

11   Follis—a French lightweight ten speed bicycle model 572.

My trust in communal housemates now shaken, when Martha invited me to dinner to socialize with Julian and his friend, I stood her up.

That night, Wilma talked about Martha. She said, "I didn't expect you to fall in love with someone older."

Martha was angry. I thought it was over, but that weekend we drove down the peninsula early in the morning to attend the workshop by the psychologists and Gary. They explained how by watching our eye movements they could tell whether we accessed our auditory, visual, or kinesthetic centers in our brains. They could tell which of these three realms were primary in any given person. By using key words, they could correct neurosis focusing linguistically on the primary realm. They told of how they wrote their book and then lost the manuscript in a fire. "We recreated it," they said. Now they were sharing the wisdom.

Martha coded as auditory and I coded kinesthetic. On a break between sessions, I socialized a little with the others at the workshop. We stood outside in the heat and I smoked a cigarette while swinging my leg against the curb. Martha did not come outside because of her cast. The others were older, and we didn't have much in common to talk about. I felt out of place and time.

I told Al and Ralph, that I wanted to become a writer. They hypnotized me, and Gary told a story about a prince, who found a magic frog under a trap door in a field. Gary entranced in an unassuming mountain twang. The prince went down many steps into a deep underground den (diving into the unconscious) and met this frog who helped him win the challenge with his brother for the King's inheritance. In the process the prince discovered a magic carpet, a stunning diamond ring, and a princess. Each in turn helped him to impress the King despite the prince looking ugly.I asked Gary what he heard when he finished writing a story. "Applause," he said.

Released from hypnosis I burst into tears.

Unsympathetic, Martha said, "go see a shrink."

The first of many to say this to me.I knew it was over. She said we had a difference in maturity.

Wilma still wanted to be a couple. Finished. I couldn't continue. I had never really seen us as a couple.

After leaving The Jewish Institute of Cincinnati, I walked four miles to the Norwood Lateral, wearing only a white T-shirt, blue jeans, and new white sneakers (I cannot remember if Mom or Dad took me to Reading road Sears & Roebuck and bought them at a moment of truce saying, "you should buy your own shoes.") I hitchhiked out I-71 to Cleveland, and on through Pennsylvania to upstate New York with only six dimes and six Buffalo nickels to my name. In Buffalo, cadged a long-necked beer in a bar then walked, found a parked car behind a long low building, wedged open the door and slept shivering in the front seat. In the dawn light began a long walk alone, played a harmonica, drifted in and out of towns and cities, feeling isolated, alienated from my peers, unlike other times, the adventure, getting high in cars, and conversing with random drivers, I felt a new pulse in America.

When I got to Cambridge, I saw a woman selling flowers in Harvard Square. Could it be Caroline Kenneney? Was she really serving tables at 33 Dunster? And did they really need a barback/busboy? Could I work my way through Harvard and stay at 3 Sacramento St? I moved in, then got kicked out of a single on the first floor where my friend Peck had stayed in 1976. Another guy, Guy, who hated me and had married my first college girl, now pregnant; they got the room despite my letter pinned to the bulletin board on the stairwell. I tried to register for classes but had a hold on my account.

After a week working late shifts at the restaurant, hauling five-gallon buckets of ice—two at a time—from the kitchen to the bar through the crowds of returning students I decided to return to Cincinnati for treatment. Messages from the Dudley Senior Tutor advised me to do so. I picked up the bicycle parts and packing from the Bursar, but I didn't have the $63.48 yet. The 33 Dunster manager wanted a Social Security number. Afraid to share it, I asked to be paid in cash. The nights had been so late that I never collected my tips. After firing me for missing the employees meeting, the manager paid me $25.00 cash. I drank a short stout without paying in a quiet moment at the bar. I knew that I had a drinking problem. Then I hitchhiked back to Cincinnati.

Outside Syracuse, New York I was picked up by police for hitchhiking.

"What are you doing here?" Asked the tall cop swaying in breezy dry leaves.

"Eating an apple." There was a tree laden with fruit.   "What are you doing here?" There were two out of the car, hands on hips, handcuffs ready.

Staring .

Silence.

"It looks like you're a vagrant."

"I'm on my way home from Harvard to Cincinnati. I had to pick up the bicycle parts and the clothes." I bit the apple, chewed sweet fruit.

"You don't belong here. We're taking you for a side trip."
Six times I'd used

Harvard to get me out of trouble, no more.

Handcuffed, put in the car, taken to the station. Plaid suitcase searched. Letter from Bursar asking for $63.48 and returning aluminum bicycle parts and clothing discovered.

"Damn, man, he is from Harvard. What's in Cincinnati?"
"Family."

Cigarette pack checked for marijuana. Questioned about French brand packet.

Returned to the highway at the edge of town.

"Get out of here. And don't come back." The laughing echoed.

△ △ △   △ △ △

This time I was locked in a room at The Jewish Institute upon arrival. When released from the locked room, I tried to show the psychiatric techs what I had done to Mom. In a lounge area I picked up a chair, held it over my head. The response was immediate and perfect. Escorted to the quiet room, put in four-point restraints and injected with Haldol. Two weeks passed, released from restraints, I pounded on and kicked walls until paint peeled and drywall broke. I COULD TRY TO APOLOGIZE FOR ALL THE WORRY, PAIN, AND AGONY, BUT WHAT GOOD WOULD IT DO? I was too angry. The nation went through far worse.

Dad came to see me, and so did his lawyer, a big man who played Judo. They called me incompetent. Trapped, without escape, enough evidence that something had gone wrong. Dressed in army surplus air force flight suit over my blue velour suit, when we got to probate court and Mom said on the witness stand that I had threatened her, I understood. My denial went deep. Gravely mentally ill, when they asked, I mustered,

"What she said is the truth."

When they forced medication after court, I fought, tearing at a man's watch, throwing punches as they cornered me in the tiny yellow cell.

The next five years I spent months at a time in psychiatric hospitals, short term and long term, private and public, as well as a year in two different group homes, one in Cowtown and one in Cincinnati. While in treatment I saw *The Deer Hunter,* starring Bobby D., Christopher Walker, and Meryl Strimp, for her a breakout film. Director Michael Cheeto used techniques inspired by television commercials to amplify the impact of the film's violence. I read about this use of technology, and comparable to my growing insight into schizophrenia, I was aware of the theory, and my knowledge had no effect on its consequences. I saw it. Illicitly hitchhiked there alone, walked back to the institution in the rain, attempted to shore myself up when in fact I carried deep competitive fear. I painted, sculpted stone, drew and wrote before I could accept the social help that my parents and the psychiatrists offered. I gradually accepted rules, and medication. I thought I could become a dentist. I enrolled at Ohio Snake Dental starting part time for about two years. I studied French, English, and studio arts. To relate my artwork to recovery frustrated me, growing my emotional resistance. The good-looking women were in therapy, and the medicine they gave me kept me zipped. I made sketches of people who helped me, including a staff worker at the group home.

He helped the residents through John Lennon's death. I didn't remember my time with John. This ambiguity within my memory began a long-standing puzzle of tropes among fellow writers. I can't remember their names.

The very good help made a difference. With the musicians, alcohol and marijuana keyed my emotive music. At the hospitals we had drug free and sober music groups. I was more comfortable with the stoned memories of making music at a bar near one institution and the recovered purple faze in

Cuba. The intimacy of sharing the stage, watching people dance and move while playing blues harmonica opened a synesthetic vein. The necessity when improvising to feel the moment, to access listening skills, and to share the mix, keep time, know when to follow, and when to lead. Influenced by strange elixirs smuggled from Colombian jungles I saw colors, felt waves, and connected telepathically. After seeing *The Deer Hunter*, I played harmonica in a bar stoned and saw Christopher Walker dancing. But I thought he was dead. Then I got an inkling I might be an actor and all I went through just a film. It was a better way to think of life. Less attached. I began to wonder which scenarios had included my death?

△ △ △   △ △ △

There were two excursions with Tom in the early 80s. When he graduated from Berkeley after working on a shrimper in Mexico cooking for, and hosting biologists and other scientists, he came to visit in the winter when I was in dental school, when I lost weight and got stable on medication prescribed by my parents' hired doctor. I think if I remember correctly, This is where we met the white Rabbit. It was either a late seventies or early eighties model with low mileage. Before that, Tom drove an old yellow Beetle which he had painted to look like a potato bug, one of the pests that had troubled Veritable Veggies. So, he came to Columbus in the Rabbit.

We went into the wilderness of Hocking Hills, hiked in the snow to the trailhead, after leaving the car at a turnaround. Our walk was mystical. Snow fell, we hiked, talked, and genuinely found ourselves in one another's company. Tom tutored me with a 60s SLR Nikon[1]. His field studies included entomology. I teased him that his interest in pest control really

---

1 Nikon—in this case actually a Nikkormat, a Japanese Single Lens Reflex film camera known for its ruggedness, manual settings, and high-quality lens. It could easily and quickly accommodate lens changes, and could be fitted for a variety of uses.

started with me. He used the camera's extension tubes to make fine photos of insects, flora, and ice formations. That day we passed the camera back and forth. When we returned to the car, it would not start. The wipers worked, the engine cranked a little, but no spark. We walked the road until we found another hiker, who took us to the nearest town. We were able to find, on New Year's Day, a working man with a truck and a tow chain. I steered the white Rabbit through the snow. The mechanic, with Tom, drove the tow vehicle, on twisty, slippery roads with windshield wipers broken, and a defroster that blew air with no heat.

In Lancaster, where we took the car, the mechanic had a woodburning stove, oil disposal barrels, Rube-Goldberg exposed wiring in a shop full of grit. He was very kind but could not make the repair. The mechanic and his wife drove us to Columbus, and we bought McD's in gratitude. I rode a Trailways bus back to Lancaster a few days later. A Rabbit Mechanic found a leak around the antenna that when warm enough, wet the fuse box, shorted the ignition, and when frozen wreaked havoc on the car's electronics. I returned the car to Cincinnati where Mom and Dad put me on the Greyhound back to Columbus before my winter break concluded.

After the next trip, I began my decline into heavy drinking my last term at the dental fraternity. The family's goal was to get Tom into the Ivy League school of his choice. I didn't much care what happened to me.

On this drive we talked about *Fenderton the Brain King*[2]. Fenderton, Fellow's naked character, had inspired thinking about who I was and what I was doing. I very much wanted to be larger than life. "How would Fenderton react to a hitchhiker?" I asked. On State Route 15 between Pennsylvania

---

2 *Fenderton the Brain King*—consider *Henderson the Rain King* by Saul Bellow.

and New York, we picked one. Tom said no, but no, then yes. The traveler liked our music, we had an eight-track player, and tuned to folk stations when we weren't listening to Marlo Dustbowl[3]. The traveler seemed to have some marijuana. I indulged and I don't remember what ensued, except for some greasy food, a laundromat in Ithaca, and sleeping in the car. Tom was gone for a day and a half, to an interview, and to teach me a lesson. I gathered I had been ill disposed. Tom eked into graduate school in the Ivy League

My other brother, Will, lived in Columbus for a time, having picked up with an ex-girlfriend from Cincinnati who attended veterinary school. She had been on the bike trip in the summer of '75. We had rivaled for her attention. We'd sailed a few times together on the Olentangy River Reservoir at Leatherlips Yacht Club. I had a friend, Kim. who owned an open boat, a Thistle[4]. Kim had biked with me from Vic Village to the lake, raced and cycled back. He lived in the dental fraternity but was an undergrad and not on the dental track. When Will sailed with us Kim let me helm. WHAT A MEMORY, the lowing of elephants from the neighboring zoo, the wind in our faces, and Will reciting *Tabbeywocky*[5].

At one point in the summer of '79, while I tried to get published in *Harpo's Magazine*, sure that this time would work, I submitted an early chapter of *Jack Acid Radio Tape* that I'd read aloud at several community writer's groups and been advised to remove the smoking scenes. There were passages detailing a hitchhiking journey, driving drunk at night, <u>smoking weed,</u> and taking Amtrak from Toledo to Boston

3   Marlo Dustbowl—a bad play on words on Arlo Guthrie.

4   Thistle—Thistle is a high-performance one-design racing sailboat that is generally sailed with a three-person crew.

5   *Tabbeywocky—Jabberwocky.*

where I met Caroline Kenneney at a party. I never got the results of this submission until I heard from the woman in Santa Fe. I had used her address.

At dental school I tried to seduce a woman writer in the summer workshop, it was the last time I would try to seduce a woman that I don't remember, strangely I have the painting of her, and still no memory. I took her to Leatherlips, and stoned, as was my habit, lost my glasses into the Olentangy. Now at night, nearly blind, and hallucinating, I saw the scene as the Mekong River, me drunk and recalling *The Deer Hunter's* violence. This attempted seduction ended in befuddlement, wasted, half-blind, scared, I slept it off somewhere unremembered.

Thankfully Will took me to the dock some days later, dove in the murky water and found my spectacles. His steadiness, his presence then, helped me more than I can express. I made a painting of the woman, which I call: Blonde Who Revels in Light. To this day it's a favorite, though I don't remember the woman's name, or even if it resembles her. The key to Blonde, these amazing gouache green eyes, and the hands pictured in a position that no one's hands could be held.

Pressed to make ledgers, by my caring mom, I listed my costs for cigarettes and alcohol, but never kept receipts and distorted the quantities. When I stopped the zippy medication, the psychiatrist, and the classes, I knew I had to make change. But I couldn't recall that resolve. I wonder if it was disulfiram (known to me as Antabuse[1]) they gave me? I had alcoholism in third stage.

There were the negotiations with professors, such as asking to write a paper rather than take a grade for an unexpected exam poorly written. (Drunk and hungover the day of the exam.) I worked with a tutor who had been a Peace Corps Volunteer and still I barely passed French Literature. Using a French/English dictionary I translated without clear understanding, misusing words á droit, et á gauche.

I was more interested in his girlfriend, whom I painted. She administrated a program that placed volunteers with developmentally disabled adults. I volunteered and rode the bus with a twenty-eight-year-old man to the downtown

---

1   Antabuse—a drug that causes an adverse reaction to alcohol.

Lazarus store so he could shop for 45's. My motivation was to see the woman administrator whose kindness made a real difference. He liked her, too. She came to the group home, let me sketch her, and when I first lived alone in the Wilber St. second floor walk-up, she came to dinner, and brought kitchenware.

As I grew more committed to isolation, and drank heavily, a bus driver paused in his day to tell of a legendary English icon who, intoxicated, offered six tickets to a tram conductor, recounting when the conductor said, "Professor Denny, you only need two. And Denny's reply, 'That's okay, I'm gonna lie down.'" I thought he was bragging on Professor Denny, I see now he planted a seed for me about my alcohol abuse. They named a building after him.

Perhaps most disturbing, I knew a Physics graduate student who gave a private demonstration of the planetarium then tried to sell me a revolver. Fear from that encounter led me to drop Social Sciences where the lecturer spoke from the stage of bringing a gun on campus. I thought about shutting out the lights in the auditorium to put a real scare into students.

The first week of winter quarter, I attended two lectures on Symbolic Logic. The Prof, a man in his fifties, explained some ideas, and I stopped by his office. He had a life size poster of Hendrix on the wall. I went back to my Wilber St. apartment, wrote a single page essay that questioned sequential logic, profoundly comparing it to poker, and claimed no abstract symbols existed in the text that could be identified as non-sequential, condensing it to conclude with a fifth (as in a fifth of alcohol) which likely came at the end of one day and the beginning of another, as to me linearity no longer held sway. The non-narrative sequence and the postmodern conceit held me unaccountable for my drunkenness. I slid my only copy of the paper under the Prof's office door, withdrew from classes, and collected refunded tuition without informing my family. GUILTY AS CHARGED.

I knew what I had done was wrong, and I spent the winter cycling, eating lox, smoking Djarum, drinking, and painting. What began as self-righteous indignation turned into a nightmare of singular insularity. I was right about everything. No one understood. This is the state where I hovered, inches above the gutter, spending with no plan, complaining over the stupidest shit.

In Spring of 1982, with no direction, no responsibilities, no commitments, I received a letter from the woman in Santa Fe, New Mexico, an ex-girlfriend twice my age. This time there were dried flowers amidst the pages. We'd met on a dance floor when I was 19, and she was 39, when I had escaped California starving from guilt related to Wilma and Martha. Something drew me to Linda. She had sent me tapes to the institution, a photo of Nityananda[1], tucked in loving letters. I decided to go see her with my remaining money, so I hitchhiked West out of Columbus. By then my phone was disconnected, and she never had a phone, so I left Columbus without reaching out. On the trip I drank and smoked pot, rides that may have ended with spiderwebbed windshields stained in blood, hallucinatory memory. The last leg of the trip from Amarillo I rode the grey dog, asking if I had been delivered by some providence to this woman's home.

When I saw her, I knelt in prayer. She was with another man, crying, and just had a biopsy for breast cancer.

Δ Δ   Δ Δ

Schizophrenia is characterized by grandiosity, delusion, hallucination, and psychosis. I have always thought of myself as important, perhaps more than necessary, and while it is difficult to prove, have had experiences with the paranormal including synesthesia, that clinicians called hallucinations,

---

1 Bhagawan Nityananda—an Indian guru of the 20th century.

and have had a history of angry outbursts, most often drug, or alcohol induced. I think some might say I use the schizo card when it is useful and deny it when it gets in the way. I take my medication daily. I experience frustrating side-effects from this. The alternative is not worthwhile.

Often people with mental illness do not believe the problem is within. A person with paranoia commonly believes the problem is with others. "You are afraid of me," therefore "I am called paranoid." This is complicated when medicine is forced on the individual, as in my case. The probate court, first at the behest of my family, and later when family gave up, at the behest of friends, mandated medication. Once the medication was started, if it were discontinued for any reason, a legal process began if my behavior warranted it. So, working closely with medical professionals was, and continued to be, necessary. Further complicating this situation is that once I felt comfortable, things were back to somewhat normal, it seemed like I could just discontinue the medication, lose weight (as antipsychotic medication led to a more sedentary existence), and regain the motivation that seemed absent. When I tried stopping the medication the result was a slow, but consistent return of the active symptoms of the illness.

Schizophrenia's symptoms are usually divided into five main categories according to the DSM-5[2]: Delusions, Hallucinations, Negative Symptoms, Disorganized Thinking, and Grossly Disorganized or Abnormal Motor Behavior. The medical model lacks the nuance and subtlety of experiential models, terms are repetitive, redundant, and contradictory. So IS MY STORY. Often with schizophrenia use of street drugs

---

2 *Diagnostic and Statistical Manual of Mental Disorders*—a publication by the American Psychiatric Association for the classification of mental disorders using a common language and standard criteria.

and alcohol to mediate symptoms further complicates the matter. Counter-culture heroes such as Yippie founder, my old acquaintance, Paul Krassner said: "I wouldn't take any drug prescribed by a doctor." Often proponents of marijuana suggest it is a natural herb, grown in soil, rather than a synthetic pill, developed in a laboratory. Even LSD comes from ergot and may have been ingested by unsuspecting villagers on spoiled rye bread at some unknown point in man's history. The literature suggests the possibility ergot poisoning could be responsible for fifteenth century witch hunts. In a film about Kesey, and the Merry Pranksters, the word "argot" is curiously interjected for "ergot."

This counterculture did have a private language, and the credo, "Never trust a Prankster." LSD has been identified as a catalyst for the onset of schizophrenia, and hallucinogens are discouraged by psychiatrists when concurrent with anti-psychotic medications. There is a category in the DSM for drug-induced psychosis.

Meditation, yoga, and a healthy diet are helpful to those with schizophrenia, however those who claim these alone will suffice to control active symptoms are in the minority. The preponderance of evidence suggests otherwise. The question of what is natural and what is not seems to have a great significance in contemporary food and medical culture.

In some sense it might be analogous to synthetic music versus acoustic music. Purists of all sorts descend on such questions with the vigor and energy of bees extracting nectar from the nether parts of a flower blossom. The consequential trembling resembles a common side-effect of haloperidol, extrapyramidal movement disorders, shaking vibration in extremities, such as feet and hands. Another medication, benztropine, is prescribed to counteract the tremors, still in my case the tremors are only reduced. While this side-effect has no judgement attached to it, the discomfort, and resulting social anxiety, having to explain, etc. generates circumstances that heighten stigma.

Similarly, schizophrenia's functional consequences vary widely. For some, when delusions are not being openly discussed, behavior and social norms are uninterrupted. However, from the first question in a social setting, "Why is your hand shaking?" Variance from an innocent social norm sends a host of signals. *Do I talk about the medication? Then what? The illness? The explanation of what it is? The personal history? What parts are going to engender interest? What if this interaction could lead to a friendship? A sexual partner? A relationship? If it is someone one isn't so attracted to, how to keep it simple?*

The tremor indicates I'm on the medicine, and when sketching, or musically feathering vibrations to color the tone of a melody, or blow great vibrato, it can be an advantage. This doesn't sound complicated at first, but boundaries in today's society are fluid. As are social lubricants. Performance enhancing drugs for artists and musicians are measured just as medicines in dental practice. Drinking for social reasons often results in social isolation. Especially when addiction becomes a problem as it did for me.

What are dating dos and don'ts for those diagnosed with schizophrenia? What are the social contracts around addiction and recovery? Is it fair to not tell? How do normal people react to the self-consciousness of someone who clearly knows he is ***different***? In a society where mental illness affects one in ten—where one in four has a family member with mental illness—does one share one's "dirt," or try to hide it? Ever heard the expression, "Sweep it under the rug?"

In my case, fortunately or unfortunately, I have some real artistic skills, real musical gifts, and can write well. I like myself. Perhaps I'm a bit self-involved, however in such a narcissistic, materialistic society, THIS IS NORMAL. I've seen the insides of some institutions and studied at seven universities. I've lived in poverty as well as relative luxury. I've performed publicly in front of large audiences, and entertained in night clubs, bars, and coffeehouses. And I've driven a Rolls-Royce, if only for five minutes! I know from experience that stealing does not pay. WHAT TO SHARE? AND WITH WHOM? AND WHEN? Culinary and bartending skills are important, too. How do you throw a sober party?

△ △ △   △ △ △

These three poems, written in the mid-nineteen-eighties when I lived in Over-the-Rhine changed my life, brought me recognition when they were published, and spoke to the general public. "Popsicle Stick" appeared in *The Art Academy News*, a monthly newspaper published by the Art Academy in Cincinnati. The other two were part of the Neighborhood Poet Laureate contest entry I sent in 1984 and 1985 respectively. I was twice named Poet Laureate of Over-the-Rhine. *The Cincinnati Enquirer Tristate Magazine*, a Sunday supplement to the daily paper carried an interview, photo, and article with some of "Main Street" in June of 1986. Two days before the article appeared, I met the woman with whom I've had my longest intimate relationship. We met at Arnold's Bar and Grill where I was a regular for years. The article helped win her. Later that summer I was admitted to The Union Institute[3], then called The Union of Experimenting Colleges and Universities, where I soon became employed as the Admissions Processor for the Union Graduate School. The Registrar who hired me had cut the poem, "Popsicle Stick", out of the newspaper and posted it in her library.

3   The Union Institute & University—Union Institute & University educates highly motivated adults who seek academic programs to engage, enlighten and empower them to pursue professional goals and a lifetime of learning, service and social responsibility.

POPSICLE STICK

There's
little
left
to kid
about
waiting
in
discouraged
faced
line
gritting
teeth
against
another
cigarette
smoked
too quickly. The

agony of
it   all
escapes
into
huffs of
white
smoke to
get foodsta
mps
under
fluoresce

nt lamps
among
the
distraug
ht   faces
of poor.
Lines.

Lines
look
like
poetry
,
impo
verish
ed on
a
page,
never
short
enoug
h   to
say in
even
breath
s,
nor long enough
t
o
l
a
s

t
a
l
l
d
a
y
.

Like a
popsicle
melting
and
falling
off   the
stick.
What's
left   to
lick tastes
like the
stick,
w
o
o
d
e
n
,
b
u
t
s

till a little bit sweet.

Δ Δ Δ   Δ Δ Δ

MAIN STREET

Shattered glass etchings on the sidewalk, broken puddles piled; scattered around ragged splintered white painted wooden window frames. Cold quart brown beer bottles paper bagged, nozzles wrapped tightly, crumpled on their sides around grey parking meters flanked by gas guzzling cars. Mercury vapor glow of night light shows locked gates. It's only 11:30 on a Wednesday, but Aunt Maudie's is closed, a tiny Master padlock invites no one to enter. The traffic lights flash yellow, an occasional car lights the way up Main Street. No sign of yesterday's warm winter weather people as rock music wafts onto the air, tonight is cold, the ones with homes are in them. Earth movers gape at the street, their yellow rusty bodies stand inert until dawn when the workmen will pour coffee out of silver thermoses into dented cups before starting the big machines that open the pavement to change the sewer lines. Then the merc vapor lights will turn off, the street barrier orange lifesaver lights will be shut out. Morning will bring buses.

The supervisor

The sarge was my super dupervisor.
He had earned two brave purple
hearts, (One more brave than the
other as he tells us.) and a bronze
star. He had a trail of stories that
filled the flesh of his arm with
tattoos; (my favorite about the time
he picketed the White House
chanting and displaying signs which
read, "A Little Piece Never Hurt
Anyone.") I exaggerate, so does he.

He wields a sweeper and a
broom over us, insisting we can
do better for ourselves and the
Hamilton County Justice
Center when we clean with our
tools of conviviality.

He has a face that has aged
and once had been partially
lifted giving his cheeks a
prominent height atypical
for a Jewish man of his age.
His pudgy body moves with authority—

as a bartender he learned to stand and
drink. Now, he abstains, speaks
loudly, echoes an era full of din,
abrupt answers, skillfully attacks then
avoids, and hammers the crew with
watered down wet clichés.

Before graduate school at Redspin University in 1999, I applied for a job, counseling inmates in a prison for non-violent offenders. The therapeutic community model suggested that when inmates misbehaved, their punishment should be to write about their behavior. This implied to me, chipping away at the structure of joyful creativity and I rejected it, chose instead to take loans and a fellowship to embrace higher education. I would teach college composition with a focus on the literature of the homeless, where academic freedom allowed me to generate curriculum with a structure and a measure of social justice. At Redspin University I would take privileged kids whose parents were paying for their education and give them some immersion experiences in Cincinnati's Over-the-Rhine. I would encourage students to write about their shoes and the shoes of others.

AFTERWORD

Would you rather hear about how I was gorked up on pills given me by a community mental health agency psychiatrist in 1985? I was taught a lesson. You, clean that baseboard, and take your time. Make it shine. I was on my knees at night in the Hamilton County Justice Center hallway, working with a rag and a bucket of soapy water. I had a spray bottle. Some of the crew were smoking pot in the bathroom. The supervisor had me on a short list of those to watch. He had been military, a sergeant with a purple heart. Recovering alcoholic, and he talked about it. Would you rather hear about how I worked for less than minimum wage, discussed my predicament, meanwhile making notes for poems? It was a training program. On the proficiency test with the vacuum in the office, I did terrible. Gorked up on pills. If I couldn't get it together to work, then the supervisor just shunted me off in an office, or the corner of a hallway, put someone near me so I didn't wander off, we could complain if we dared. Then he had to get the place clean enough to meet the Deputies' standards. The Deputies in the lock-up visiting area buzzed us in with our cleaning supplies, taunted us on the PA system while we mopped and wiped baby shit off the fixed shiny stainless-steel stools. The stink, I remember. Even gorked up, I could smell shit.

After we worked, we walked down to Ronald's. Stood at the bar among the huddled artists. Talked to butchers, painters, cabinetmakers, and listened to the singers, watched the floozies dance, and the dancers floozy. One could say we were America then. No fuckin' tv in that bar.

When I turned 23 in 1981, I knew I had to make a decision whether to live in Columbus, finish my undergraduate degree at The Ohio State University, with the support of my parents or to move on. By then my seventeen-month older brother was enrolled in a Masters degree at Cornell, and presumably was stable enough to support himself. He had been given a car, and with time would be backed financially to buy a trailer with his partner. I had a long-distance relationship with an older partner in Santa Fe, New Mexico and had not succeeded in building a promising future with a woman I met in Worthington, Ohio.

After three years of mental health treatment, I stopped taking the antipsychotic medication prescribed for two years. My drinking increased, spending time in bars on High Street, and consuming wine at my Victorian Village apartment. My days split between painting and cycling. I enjoyed feeling my physical strength increase as the tranquilizing medication left my system. I worked on a painting that was intended to be a mural someday, six figures, each torn from some part of my past, with the characters bringing a gift to a half-circle under a gas lantern suspended above them. Some fifteen years later, the piece would be framed and hanging in the entryway of my Clifton apartment, and Brett Dillingham, a childhood friend, on a brief visit, gave it a title: Six Waiting for a Seventh, You the Viewer. To this day the mural dream, borrowed from the fictional Gulley Jimson, has not been realized.

The trip to see Linda in Santa Fe, hitchhiking and on the gray dog, took me to new limits. Fortunately, or unfortunately memories of those times reside in a haze of brown outs, and black outs, along with painful scenes that host trauma. A bloody spiderwebbed windshield, a burly bearded man in a sleeveless shirt with a double-bitted axe climbing out of a truck, and me standing disoriented on a dark highway nursing hooch. Somehow in Amarillo I found the bus station and got to Santa Fe. Linda was the first of my dear close ones that I lost. My schizophrenia and alcoholism, her cancer, a vivid concoction of poison.

After returning by bus to the Midwest, I stayed in Columbus until the eviction order scared me out. I had no money, was frightened and isolated, had no real plan, so on Memorial Day weekend 1982, I bicycled to Cincinnati overnight. I slept on the apron of a gas station in Lebanon where I got disoriented in the dark. In the morning I made my way down through Fort Ancient, and Oregonia, climbing the long winding hill to find my way into the Ohio River Valley. Once in Cincinnati, I visited a few familiar places before flatting my tires, and leaving the bicycle on my parents' front porch.

Soon I wandered the streets of Clifton, dressed in a rust-colored wool sweater, wool cycling shorts, leather, cleated, cycling shoes, and a red and black bike cap. When I encountered people I recognized, I asked for money, went into several of the bars on McMillan and Ludlow, got drunk, snuck into unlocked buildings on the University of Cincinnati campus, and even a neighborhood church looking for a place to sleep it off. I walked the streets, a pauper, aimless, but knowing that I had taken the artwork and writings that were of most value to the psychiatrist's office in Worthington, Ohio and left them with the secretary. All this time I felt a great man such as me, from a neighborhood like Clifton, would find a way to recover. I knew I was penniless. The alcohol numbed me, and I felt good, gritty, angry, and justified in my anger. When I was intoxicated, I didn't have many angry encounters. I was on the streets for three to five weeks, I'm not sure exactly. My family doctor's wife visited me on a park bench, as did a childhood friend, and the doctor's wife's brother-in-law, a social worker and renowned photographer who told me I was brilliant like my father, had made a start at Harvard, and uttered the enigmatic statement, "You know why you are here." These two encouraged me. They asked me to sign myself in to the state hospital. I eventually did. By that time, I had a broken wrist, a punctured eardrum, and I found out much later, pneumonia. I knew I was very sick. The staff had decided to force medicate me, and I relented, agreed to take pills, which for the most part I have done daily since then. I had spent a night in the city jail for trespassing in the UC Law Library that was under construction. Many years later I would show some of my art there in an exhibit of mental health consumers. Some of the art I showed there in 1998 was in Worthington, Ohio at the psychiatrist's office in 1982 unframed. In 1984 I spent another night in jail on the warrant from the trespassing, when interrupted necking in Mt. Storm Park after hours with Marlena. Thus, I had a host of memories and experiences in Clifton that blended with childhood times and left me wiser when I finally settled down and stopped drinking in 1989.

In 1989 I began my career in the service of the mentally ill. I had been a complainant, a client worker, lived in subsidized housing on welfare doing volunteer work, and had survived psychiatric inpatient, halfway house outpatient, and now lived in the poorest neighborhood with an enclave of artists, musicians, dancers, writers, as well as artisans, actors, and dope dealers. I had played harmonica blues weekly at a downtown club in exchange for beverages. I sat in with a jazz trio fronted by a black woman singer who knew, but knew, she was a diva! I was lonely, and the keys player, a high school friend had met a dancer choreographer in New York, brought her back to Cincinnati to have babies, and found me, strung out, in partial recovery, and recruited me to live in the third-floor walk-up under the dance studio. I was still pretty crazy, making art, writing my first novel, Jack Acid, immersed in a study of meditation guided by a disciple of Nisargadatta. Marlena enticed me out to bowling alley bars in Covington, Kentucky where her uncle owned a lucrative printing business, had his own limousine and driver, and while she looked down on him from her position as a social worker, she oiled me with alcohol. Word was, he had ties to the Mafia. After we split, I found a writing mentor who taught at the Union Institute where I made good on my experiences in staged recovery, gaining college credit for life experience. In 1988 I graduated then rose from playpoet janitor, musician, actor, playwright, artist, to broadcaster, finding jobs as a social worker and University English tutor that allowed me to be helpful in some cases to those on similar paths to mine as well as helping ESL students.

The volunteer work I did during the early stages of my outpatient recovery included public relations writing for The Jewish Hospital of Cincinnati, The American Israelite, and teaching English as a Second Language to new arrivals and refugees in downtown Cincinnati at Traveler's Aide-International Institute. Working with an editor and teaching second grade English to adults whose Aid to Families with Dependent Children was contingent on their taking classes while my General Assistance was contingent on my volunteer position. This was during the Reagan Era, when there wasn't much money for social services, and corporate welfare helped participants in the system. Young people with addictive habits were shunned, warehoused, and yet, here I was, having started at Harvard College, essentially working for nothing doing service in the USA inner-city.

As an artist and writer, I knew the value of my work, I had seen art on the walls of Hughes High School by Frank Duveneck that inspired me. In my final weeks at Hughes, I took an exam in the library and marveled at the portrait over the door. Going to galleries and museums, family friends who were artists, art history interested me, and for me art became a big part of my personal image and imagination. As I studied the lives of artists and writers, my self-interest, my self-centeredness, imitating wanton ways described in books and films drew my eager mind. Family life lost value. I remember a couple of days hitchhiking from Columbus to Cincinnati, surprising my parents by raiding their freezer and taking a pork roast, as well as beer from the fridge, then ducking out the door and hitching back to Columbus, the roast thawed by the time I got home some eighteen hours later. This was not art, this was defiance, as I had agreed to stop hitchhiking when I went into treatment and accepted support to go to Ohio State and live in Victorian Village.

Thankfully, I survived these antics. And the difficult times moved me to meditate, move away from drama to find quiet corners. In the spotlight on stage playing harmonica fronting a loud blues band was an escape. Performing poetry at large gatherings and on the radio led to enjoying the sound of my own voice enough to record Jack Acid as a six-and-one-half hour audio novel. It circulated the way the technology allowed. First in three-hole binders, then on cassettes recorded off FM radio, and when I lost the radio show in 1998 there was a hiatus. In 2004, I regrouped, found a design team, recording engineers, and musicians to create a DIY six-cd box set with accompanying booklet. I built these one at a time, kidding that I was a factory worker at Middleton for years, then opted for a download service, which resulted in the product arriving on Spotify, with a link on my website some twenty-two years after the final version was recorded. The project begun in Palo Alto, CA circa 1976, perhaps it will be in print someday before too long.

STEVEN PAUL LANSKY
December 2021.

STEVEN PAUL LANSKY wrote *Main St.* (2002) and *Eleven Word Title for Confessional Political Poetry Originally Composed for Radio* (2009), published by Seaweed Sideshow Circus. His audionovel *Jack Acid* (2004) is available on Spotify. His memoir: *The Break* (Arbitrary Press 2022) had chapters previously published under the title: the citizen, in *The Brooklyn Rail* (2005), *ArtSpike, CityBeat, Streetvibes* and *Article 25*. His animated videos: *Bratwurst* (with Leigh Waltz), *Exit Strategy, Harvest,* and *The Broken Finger Episode A-8 or the Cigarette Break* are on YouTube channel: lanskysp. For more: *Whole Terrain, New Flash Fiction Review, Black Clock 20*, and *St. Petersburg Review Issue 8.5.* The novella, *A Black Bird Fell Out of the Sky* was published on Seaweed Sideshow Circus (2017). *Life is a Fountain*, a collection of vignettes and sketches was published by Dos Madres Press in 2018. Published under the heteronym, Paul Thanas, and illustrated by Steven Paul Lansky, *And Then the Cow Was Drownded* (2024) is his latest novel on Arbitrary Press. Original art, links to writings, the music of Lansky's harmonica heteronym, Flem Snopes and other tidbits are all at www.stevenpaullansky.com

Author photo: Robert Flischel

Other books by Steven Paul Lansky
published by Dos Madres Press

Life is a Fountain (2018)

For the full Dos Madres Press catalog:
www.dosmadres.com